DANGEROUS ENCOUNTER

RILEY EDWARDS

Dangerous Encounter
TAKEBACK 4

Cover design: Lori Jackson Designs

Written by: Riley Edwards

Published by: Riley Edwards/Rebels Romance

Edited by: Rebecca Hodgkins

Proofreader: Julie Deaton

Book Name: Dangerous Encounter

Paperback ISBN: 978-1-951567-28-6

First edition: August 30, 2022

To my family - my team – my tribe.
This is for you.

1

THERE I WAS, standing in a beautiful mansion, surrounded by beautiful people all in varying degrees of undress, watching them mingle and converse. And I was wondering not for the first time or the third or the tenth, how on earth was this my life.

I'd been to enough of these *soirées* that the nudity didn't bother me. At first, it did, until I came to the realization that the members of Club Joi paid a hefty price to be there. They paid for the opportunity and the privacy to safely and willingly participate in a lifestyle they enjoyed.

However, as the nights progressed into the public sex, I found any reason I could to leave the area. It wasn't that it was a free-for-all wild orgy. Everything revolved around consent and that included touching as well as watching. No one was forced to watch. There were designated spaces throughout the mansion where sex acts could be viewed, but no place else.

So, when the penises and vaginas came out, I skedaddled.

I actually knew how this had become my life. Every time I walked into my apartment and didn't see my room-mate's smiling, pretty face I was reminded. What I was really wondering was why on earth I thought I could find out what happened to Elise. I'd been a part-time waitress, part-time event planner for God's sake. I had no idea what I was doing or what I was looking for. It wasn't like during cocktail hour one of the members was going to announce they'd kidnapped my friend. Or during an orgasm, someone was going to scream, "Oh, yes, so good! I killed Elise Keller and buried her in the backyard."

I'd been working at Club Joi as the executive event coordinator for over six months and I hadn't heard Elise's name uttered once. At first, this made me ultra-suspicious—now I understood it was part of the respect and privacy the members extended to each other. There was zero gossip at the club. Which was frustrating. No one asked questions, more frustration.

Six months of nothing.

Elise was gone without a trace. The police were scratching their heads with no leads. Her parents were beside themselves with worry and heartbreak. And I was destroyed.

"Excuse me." A smooth, rich voice pulled me from my thoughts.

I pulled my gaze from the scantily dressed women drinking champagne in front of the fireplace in the great room to a man who interrupted my thoughts.

Adam Newcomb.

The man was a real-life, walking, talking, billboard ad for something manly.

It was a shame he was a member of a sex club. If I'd met

him out in the real world I would've done something outrageous to catch his attention, and if that didn't work, I would've approached him and asked him out for a drink.

Sandy-brown hair, nice eyes, carried himself with an air of confidence. Not the kind that was cocky and screamed douchebag. His came from someplace deep, he was comfortable in any environment. He was the master of his universe, and that was because he was good at what he did and knew it.

He was sexy as hell.

But he belonged to a sex club and that was a hard pass.

"Hello, Mr. Newcomb. Is everything all right?"

"I was going to ask you the same thing."

He was?

"Everything is wonderful, is it not?"

I glanced around the room. Everyone was smiling and happy. Having a good time talking to their fellow members, enjoying light hors d'oeuvres and the two-glass maximum for those who would be playing later. There were also strict rules about intoxication, and a drink limit for anyone who was participating in any kind of sex.

"It is," he confirmed. "That's why I'm wondering why you're standing off to the side, frowning. Do you find something particularly distasteful or is it the party as a whole?"

Damn.

Shit.

"Of course I don't find consenting adults participating in activities that are mutually satisfying distasteful. If I was frowning, I apologize, I was thinking about the champagne. More to the point, if the staff had ordered enough."

Semi-lie.

I didn't find it distasteful per se, it just wasn't my scene.

And it was not something I wanted to witness or be a part of.

Adam leaned closer, his mouth dangerously close to touching my ear when he whispered, "That sounds rehearsed." I felt his breath against my neck, I caught the scent of his woodsy cologne, and against my will, I shivered. "Or more to *my* point, it sounds like bullshit."

He straightened and I felt that, too. The loss of his closeness. It was only for a second, but I didn't miss the way his heat had surrounded me.

I tipped my head back to catch his gaze and vehemently deny his accusation. That denial was swept away by his smile. I couldn't muster any of the professionalism I'd mastered over the months I'd worked here. My resolve was slipping faster than I could remind myself that Adam Newcomb liked watching and having public sex. Not that I'd ever witnessed this firsthand. I'd never seen him bring a date, which as a top-level member he was welcome to do. I'd never seen him wander back into the viewing rooms or even sit in the lower lounge, which was referred to as the Hunting Ground, because that was where either unattached female members went to find a partner for the evening, or couples went to find a third or swap. Negotiations happened down there. And other than his tour of the property and the rooms, I hadn't seen Adam use any of the amenities.

Strange.

"Perhaps I should ask *you* if you find Club Joi distasteful," I returned.

In the last couple of months, I'd become an expert on body language, so I didn't miss the stiffness in Adam's shoulders or the way he tensed.

"Why would you ask that?"

"You've been here over two months," I noted. "Have you not found our club acceptable? Is there something I could provide for you that would make your time enjoyable?"

Holy shit.

There were some things that, when thought in your mind, sounded better than when actually spoken out loud.

I felt my face heat.

Sweat trickled between my boobs that were pushed together to the max by a fabulous but expensive bra that made them look at least a cup size bigger. I had more cleavage on display than I ever would in my real life. Though, in real life, I also didn't wear low-cut cocktail dresses and high heels.

"If I thought for a second you were offering what it sounded like you were, I would take you up on it in a hot minute. However, to answer your question, the club is perfectly acceptable."

I didn't know what to say to that. I wanted to offer what it sounded like I was. And I would be offering it if he wasn't a member. As a part of my employment contract, I had the same membership Adam had purchased. I could participate any time I wanted.

"Have a good night, Sloane."

I was still recovering from the sexy way my name had fallen from his lips, wondering how it would sound while we were in bed, naked, and he was deep inside of me, when I felt the faintest brush of his hand against mine.

Barely a brush.

But forbidden.

That slightest touch without my permission could get him banned.

His eyes danced with a dare. A naughty, filthy dare.

"You as well, Adam."

His lips quirked up into the hottest smirk that made my thighs squeeze together.

That smirk turned primal.

And I had a feeling I'd unwittingly issued a challenge.

2

I STEPPED out into the bright SoCal sunshine, slid my sunglasses down over my eyes, and stopped dead. Not only did my feet stop moving but my heart did this funny flutter —a cross between skipping a beat and thumping double time.

Adam Newcomb.

Right in front of me.

A man who was so insanely gorgeous that it was actually annoying. I'd never seen him in the light of day, nor had I ever seen him outside of the club. And seeing him now, dressed casually with the sun's rays making his sandy-brown hair look more sandy than brown, I wished I never had. In the club, he looked like the wealthy businessman he was. In broad daylight standing on Ventura Boulevard, he looked like the quintessential California Abercrombie model and that was annoying, too. But his unruly hair, jeans that were faded in a way that let my practiced eye know they were not designer but fit him like they were specifically made for him, and his tee that molded to his upper body to perfection were not annoying—they were infuriating.

He was so freaking hot, I was rooted to the sidewalk outside of a boutique. It'd be a miracle if there wasn't drool leaking from the corner of my mouth.

Gah.

Why?

Why did hot guy Adam Newcomb have to be a member of a sex club?

Seriously!

"Sloane." My name rolled off his tongue and that was maddening, too.

There was an arrogance to the way his lips formed my name, the way his eyes danced with humor. He knew I was stunned by his presence, and he had no qualms calling me out on my stupor by way of saying my name in a sexy, smooth tone that made me wish I could hear him when we were not on a busy sidewalk but instead alone in a room with a bed and rumpled sheets after he'd given me multiple orgasms and I'd returned the favor.

Yep. That was what I was thinking, and I knew that even though my eyes were covered by my shades, Adam read my look. Those delicious lips quirked up into a smirk. And you guessed it, that smirk was sexy as fuck. I also wanted to wipe the grin off his smug—but handsome—face.

Adam's head tilted to the side just a smidge and he looked like he was going to say something. Something likely to embarrass me, like calling me out for standing there like a zombie staring at him. Or maybe he'd snap his fingers in front of my face to pull me from my dirty thoughts.

Gah.

So, I beat him to it and asked, "What are you doing here?"

The smirk turned into a full-fledged smile when he asked back, "Here, like in front of," he paused and his eyes flicked to the sign behind me, "Reclaimed? Or here as in walking down Ventura?"

"Here, as in The Valley," I clarified.

"Did I miss the sign on PCH declaring *The Valley* off-limits from all non-residents?"

I didn't miss the emphasis on "The Valley" or the snark he'd injected into his question.

"The mere fact you drove down PCH to get to Encino is grounds to kick you out."

"And which way do you prefer, Sloane?"

You bending me over the arm of my couch, pulling my hair while you take me rough.

There it was again, my name purred in a way that reminded me I was sex-starved and deprived of human touch. It was a sad time in my life. There were numerous reasons for this—the first and most important was my best friend was missing. Gone. Vanished. Without a trace. And when the days had slipped into weeks, then weeks into months and the police had no leads, no direction, no answers, my worry had turned into desperation. That desperation and fear had led me to work at a club I knew Elise had frequented. I never understood the appeal of public sex—having it or watching it. But I did understand what two or three or five consenting adults do sexually is none of my business and seeing as that was the case, my friend's sex life was not for me to judge.

Elise was sweet, loyal, outgoing, and kind. As the saying went, she'd never met a stranger. She lit up every room she entered. She made everyone around her smile. She was also too trusting and more than a little naïve. Not to further stereotypes, but she was the stereotypical midwestern girl who'd moved to L.A. with big dreams. She didn't want to be a model or an actress. She was perfectly content being a waitress at a high-end, trendy eatery in The Palisades where she made a good living that afforded her to live the dream she'd dreamt—a life surrounded by beauty. From the weather to the people, to the beaches, to the cityscapes Elise loved SoCal. As cliché as it was, this dream stemmed from 90's TV shows. And up until a few months ago, she was enjoying her life to the fullest. Now she was...gone.

A far step down from my friend missing, but still adding to my sadness, was that my life was no longer mine. Worry and fear and the need to find out what happened to Elise had taken over every aspect of my life. I wasn't complaining; I'd gladly put my life on hold forever if it meant I'd find Elise unharmed and alive, but still. Every waking moment was dedicated to the task of finding my friend and that included working in a sex club. My other friends drifted away. They did it slowly, as nicely as one could do while they turned their back on you, but the bottom line was that none of them understood what they called an obsession. They all thought I should get on with my life and let the police look for Elise.

As if that was going to happen.

Another step down was dating. I was not the type of woman who approached dating as a necessary evil or the path to finding a husband. I loved *dating*. I loved the thrill of meeting someone new. I loved the getting-to-know-you part. I loved going out and having fun, getting wild, loud, and crazy. I loved that when I was older and settled, I'd have a million great stories to tell. I loved my life—scratch that; before Elise disappeared, I loved my life. Now my every thought was consumed with horrid, scary thoughts about what could've happened to her. Where she was. What *was* happening to her. The torturous thoughts were never-ending.

Unless Adam Newcomb was in my line of sight.

Then all I could think about was how disappointing it was I'd never have a chance to find out if he could be wild, crazy, loud, and fun.

Sex club.

He belonged to a sex club and that was a hard pass.

When it came to sex, I was adventurous, but not *that* adventurous.

"Sloane?"

Darn. Why do I turn stupid around this man?

"Decker to the One-Oh-One," I answered. "Or Kanan to the One-Oh-One. Never PCH, that's for tourists."

Adam almost looked disappointed I didn't respond in kind to the innuendo he threw my way.

There was a stretch of silence that was so awkward I debated turning on my fabulous wedge sandals—that I got on discount, thus I couldn't pass them up even if I owned five other similar pairs—and running. Okay, I wouldn't've actually run, I would've walked quickly in an effort to flee from the uncomfortableness. Not to mention, Adam's gaze had turned assessing. He'd gone from cocky-playful to intense. So intense I found myself wanting to shift my weight from foot to foot under his heavy scrutiny.

"I'd better—" I started but didn't finish because Adam started at the same time and talked over me. "Do you work tonight?"

I felt my shoulders tense and that tightness spread fast, like wildfire, until every inch of me was strung taut. There was something about this handsome, sophisticated man asking me if I was going to work that made me feel dirty.

No, filthy.

Elise.

I was doing this for Elise, I reminded myself, and let go of the breath I'd been holding.

"The club's closed tonight." I told him something he already knew.

"And?" he prompted. "You're the event coordinator. I assume it takes time to...coordinate."

Gah.

I didn't want to have a conversation about my employment out in the open on a busy sidewalk. Actually, I didn't want to have a conversation about my job duties *ever*.

"It does," I confirmed.

"So? Do you work tonight?"

"Why?"

I hadn't meant for my question to come out as snappy as it had, but I was uncomfortable and more than a little irritated that a man as sexy as Adam was not available to me.

I wasn't blind, I owned a mirror. I knew I wasn't hard on the eyes. This was not me being conceited, it was me being a woman who knew her worth and knew it extended far beyond my looks, but they definitely contributed. I also knew in the land of tanned, toned, beauty queens I was average at best. I blended in with all the rest of the women and I was more than okay with that. I didn't need to rely on the superficial to find a man to date. Further from that, I'd caught Adam staring at me in the club. He'd made his interest known and that only added to my annoyance.

His lips twitched before he said, "Because I want to ask you out to dinner."

Whoa, Nelly.

I didn't want to say what I had to say next, but I had no choice, and it royally sucked.

"I don't date men who belong to the club."

Adam blinked before he smiled wide. It was a bold,

blinding, beautiful smile. It was also different than the smiles he'd given me thus far. This one was not cocky-sure. It wasn't confident. It wasn't a flirty smirk. It was pure arrogance. It was the smile of a man who had an ace in his back pocket and he was ready to pull it out.

"I see you find that disappointing. However, I wasn't asking you on a date. I was asking you to dinner to discuss a party...well, a get-together I'm hosting. My partner is coming to California, and I'd like to put together a meet and greet for potential clients. Since I've seen your work firsthand, I thought you'd be the perfect person for the job."

Shit.

Had I totally misread the banter? The brush of his hand the last time I saw him. The way he smiled at me before he'd walked away, daring me to challenge him.

Shit.

"I...um..." I stuttered, struggling to find an excuse to turn him down.

"I was thinking something intimate. Relaxed but elegant. The guest list will be small. Fifteen people max."

I could do that in my sleep.

"What do you say? Have dinner with me tonight. I'll tell you my ideas, you can shoot them all down because they're going to be terrible, then you can wow me with your brilliance."

I had no doubt his ideas would be horrendous, and they'd probably include topless servers holding platters of pigs in a blanket.

Jeez, when had I become so judgmental?

"I'll pay you five thousand dollars. Twenty-five hundred for your expertise, twenty-five hundred if you promise to attend the event."

His offer pissed me off. More than that it made me feel icky, seriously icky.

"I'm not for sale, Mr. Newcomb," I spat.

It happened quickly, so fast that if I'd blinked, I would've missed the change. But change he did. Adam had gone from carefree to lethal in a nanosecond.

"I did not, nor would I ever infer *you* were for sale," he growled, and holy shit but against my will, I shivered at the gravel in his voice. "You're a businesswoman, your time and talent are what's for sale. My offer was meant to communicate I value your time and I appreciate your talent and I'm willing to pay you for both."

Shit, I'd misread the situation again.

"I'm sorry. I thought—"

"I know what you thought," Adam cut me off. "I am not that man."

What did that mean? He wasn't that man.

I might've assumed the worst and falsely thought he was propositioning me like I was a prostitute, however, in my very weak defense, he did belong to a club where he essentially paid to watch and have sex.

Okay, that was pushing it. What Adam actually paid for was privacy and the freedom to be who he was without judgment. And there I was being a judgmental bitch, again.

That wasn't cool.

That wasn't who I was, and I needed to rein in my critical thoughts about a man I knew nothing about.

Not only had my attitude and comments—albeit most of them internal—been uncool but Adam Newcomb was a member of Club Joi. I couldn't afford to get fired, which was exactly what would happen if Adam complained about me to my boss.

So I did something I didn't want to do and I did it with a fake smile plastered on my face.

I accepted.

"Where would you like to meet for dinner?"

He didn't gloat, he didn't smirk, he didn't so much as grin when he asked, "Do you live at the beach or near here?"

Fuck.

"I live near here, but I have no problem driving to the beach if you prefer."

He pulled out his wallet, fished out a business card, and held it out.

"You pick," he told me when I took the card. "I'm available any time after seven. Text me where and I'll make a reservation." He paused and leveled me with an intense stare that made my belly feel funny. "I really hope you text, Sloane. But if you don't, no hard feelings. Understand?"

He was leaving the ball in my court and wouldn't complain to my boss if I didn't call.

"Understand."

"Sorry to have held you up. Have a great rest of your day shopping."

With that, he strolled away.

I watched him go for longer than I should have, and I did it with my eyes alternating between his ass and taking in the way his t-shirt stretched across his wide shoulders.

He had a great walk.

He had an even better ass.

I could do this.

I could have dinner with a handsome man who was off-limits, and I could work with him to plan an event.

It would be hell, but so was the rest of my life.

3

"I THINK she's trying to kill you," Cole said from the passenger seat as I rolled to a stop at the bottom of Decker Canyon. "And by *you* I mean *us*."

I had to admit, the hairpin turns and heavy grade through the Santa Monica Mountains were a little dicey, but it wasn't death-defying.

"Damn, brother, I didn't know you were squeamish."

"Squeamish? I counted five rusted-out carcasses of cars down in the ravine. And it's a long drop, friend. A long, terrifying, ass-puckering drop."

"How do you manage to live in Idaho?" I asked as I waited for the traffic to clear.

Once the traffic broke and I had a clear shot, I swung left onto Pacific Coast Highway and headed south toward our rental, which incidentally was fifteen miles down PCH from the eleven-thousand-square-foot Malibu mansion that was home to Club Joi.

The rental my boss, Wilson McCray, managed to snag wasn't eleven thousand square feet, but it was a multi-million-dollar, luxury home with a kickass deck that overlooked the Pacific. And I was pretty sure I saw Dustin Hoffman walking his dog along the surf just that morning while I was sitting on a lounger drinking coffee. In other words, the two-thousand-square-foot home on Broad Beach might not be a mansion, but it was Charlie Harper swank. It was also a necessity. It wouldn't do for a rich businessman to live in a shithole. And for this assignment that was what I was, a rich businessman with a kink—the kind that only Club Joi could provide.

"I live in Idaho under duress," Cole groused. "If I didn't totally dig Brooklyn and think Remy's the shit, I would've protested our move from Arizona."

Brooklyn was my teammate Rhode Daley's fiancée and Remington was their son. A son Rhode didn't know existed until a job took us to Spokane, Washington. Normally a situation such as this would be fucked, but Brooklyn didn't hide her pregnancy or hide Remy from Rhode. She simply couldn't find him to tell him that their no-name-night-of-fun in a Washington D.C. hotel room had resulted in Remy. From the moment Rhode found out about Remy, he was all-in. And not just with getting to know his son and helping to raise him but winning Brooklyn over. Thankfully he accomplished both those tasks. So when Takeback was faced with losing Rhode or moving the operation from Arizona to North Idaho where Brooklyn and Remy lived to keep Rhode, Wilson made the right decision to keep the team together and move headquarters to Coeur d'Alene, Idaho. I personally preferred the mild summers of North Idaho to the feel of my skin melting off in the desert. I also preferred the lush-green and beautiful lakes to Southern California traffic and smog.

But living in a beach house for a spell certainly didn't suck.

"Though," Cole continued, "nothing beats SoCal women." His neck was craned to the right and he was staring out the window at two women walking down the side of the highway with wetsuits pulled down to their hips, bikini tops visible, carrying boards.

Before I could stop it, a ridiculous image of Sloane popped into my head, and I wondered if she knew how to surf. I doubted it, which was insane to think because I didn't know the woman. I knew her credit score, I knew she rented an apartment in Encino. I knew she drove a Subaru Crosstrek and not because I'd seen it at the mansion. I also knew she was an only child, and her parents were divorced. I knew her work history, her high school GPA, and that she dropped out of CSUN after one year.

What I didn't know was her personality, not her likes or dislikes, why her parents got divorced, or why she stopped going to CSUN. Everything I knew about Sloane was from reports I'd read or the times I'd seen her while she was working. So I had nothing to base my opinions on except for a gut feeling. And my gut told me Sloane wasn't a beach girl, she'd dig the mountains. She'd get off on the beauty. But more, she'd like the challenge of the hike to get to the summit.

I shouldn't have been thinking about surfing or hiking or what the pretty woman looked like in the morning. And I certainly shouldn't have been thinking I'd seriously like to know what she looked like tangled in my sheets after I fucked her rough. I wanted to know everything about Sloane and not because it was my job to get close to her. Sure, I wanted to know why the fuck she was working at a sex club when she very obviously found it distasteful. I wanted to know why she'd quit her job as an event planner at a large management company to work for Club Joi. Why she left a waitressing gig she worked three days a week when she'd made decent money. She wasn't rolling in it, but she was far from hurting. Her bills were paid, her car paid off, money in savings. So why the hell was Sloane working in a sex club when it was obvious she didn't have a taste for kink?

Club Joi wasn't my scene, it was my assignment. I wasn't a fan of watching live-action porn being played out in front of me and it was apparent Sloane wasn't a fan either. She studiously avoided the playrooms; I no longer had that luxury if I wanted to keep my cover. The first few weeks, I had a plausible excuse; I was getting the lay of the land. Now, I had to wander in and out of the rooms and watch, especially since it would be a cold day in hell before I'd publicly fuck a woman. There was a lot I would sacrifice for an investigation, but performing or allowing sex acts to be performed on me was a line I wouldn't cross.

But Sloane was never in those rooms. She always stuck to the large upstairs living space or the kitchens and sent one of her staff into the rooms to check on members. She was polite, always. She played the part well. But she was not happy to be surrounded by naked people fucking.

Something was off and I hoped like fuck the bad feeling I had in the pit of my stomach was wrong. Club Joi was under investigation by the US Marshals Sex Offender Investigative Operations Branch for suspected human trafficking. In recent years the SOIB had been involved in a number of takedowns, so many they needed outside help to keep up with the traffickers, and that was where Takeback came in. There were a lot of foul, disgusting parts of my job. Shit that even the best horror writer couldn't possibly imagine. Sheer evil. Revolting. Shit that gave me nightmares.

I was pulled from my thoughts when my work phone

beeped with an incoming text alert. Cole snatched it out of the cupholder and helped himself to the message.

"She said she'll meet you at eight-thirty."

My pulse jumped and my fingers tightened around the steering wheel.

"Did she say where?"

"The Valley." I didn't have to look at Cole to hear the smirk in his tone. "Looks like you'll be headed back over Pucker Canyon."

Fuck.

It had been nearly three hours since I'd "accidentally" run into Sloane while she was shopping. I was lucky she'd texted me at all after I'd nearly fucked up and had to scramble and come up with something plausible on the fly to get her to go to dinner with me after she told me she didn't date men from the club. But the more I thought about it, this plan was better. I could still get close to her without doing it in a way that would fuck her over when the investigation was done. I wouldn't have to worry about hurting her. I could get to know her while she planned a fake party and when the time was right offer her protection from whoever was forcing her to work at Club Joi.

And that was what I'd concluded—Sloane didn't quit her jobs to work at a sex club because she woke up one morning and thought to herself, "Hey, I want to go watch people fuck and be miserable while doing it." Not Sloane. I didn't need to know her personally to know the woman wouldn't purposefully put herself in an uncomfortable position, and she was uncomfortable as fuck at the club.

No one else on my team agreed with me. Wilson wanted Sloane under surveillance. Cole had sided with Wilson. Reese, Davis, Jack, and Rhode who were all back in Idaho with only the reports to go by agreed with Wilson and Cole. From the outside, I understood why they'd want me to dig deeper into the mystery of Sloane. But none of them had spent time with her. None of them had watched her. None of them witnessed the unease in her eyes.

"I'll drop you off and head back over," I told Cole.

"You want cover?"

Hell no, I didn't want Cole tagging along, listening from a nearby table.

"Not necessary."

"You said she told you she didn't date men from the club," Cole began, and I already knew I wasn't going to like where that statement was going to lead. "Take her to dinner and talk about this party you need planned. I'll stop by your table and play the part of the friend who happened to be dining at the same restaurant, and you make the introductions. I'll ask her out. We can work this two ways."

Fuck no.

Hell to the motherfucking no.

Hard fucking pass.

Never going to happen.

The thought of Cole asking Sloane out made my jaw clench. The thought of Sloane saying yes made my gut roil.

"What makes you think she'd say yes?"

"Brother."

That was all my friend said and really it said it all. Cole Keniston didn't get turned down. All the more reason to keep him away from Sloane.

"Not gonna happen."

It was unfortunate I was unable to keep the indignation at bay—my tone clearly gave away my disdain, which gave Cole the opening I knew he was waiting for.

"It's been months, Asher. Maybe it's time you hand Sloane off."

Hand Sloane off?

Not gonna happen.

I then decided to verbalize my thoughts to make it crystal clear where I stood.

"Not gonna happen."

"Ash—"

"Sloane isn't a suspect. She isn't a mark. I keep telling you this and you're not getting it, brother. I'll get close, get what we need, but I'll be doing that gently. And I'll be doing it looking out for her."

"You think I'd fuck her over if she's innocent?" Cole snapped.

No, I knew he'd fuck her a different way if given the chance.

Not that I blamed him. Sloane was a beautiful woman, but it wasn't her looks that drew me to her. It was the way she carried herself with a perfect measure of confidence and apprehension. From what I'd seen she was not shy by any stretch, but she was reserved. She was watchful in a vigilant way. When she entered a room, she commanded attention whether she wanted it or not; her presence was impossible to ignore. And the more I watched her—and I'd watched closely—the more my need to know her grew. I had no claim to the woman but the mere thought of Cole touching Sloane made me homicidal. It also made my chest burn—a reaction I was trying to ignore.

And that right there should've been all I needed to back away and admit Cole was right, it was time I stepped back.

I was in too deep with a woman I knew nothing about.

"Don't say stupid shit. You know I know you better than that," I fumed. "I'm working this, and I need you to trust I know what I'm doing."

There was a beat of silence before Cole returned, "Now

who's talking stupid shit? This isn't about trust, Asher. This is about looking out for a brother when he's drowning in a woman who's tangled up in something unknown. I get you're adamant she's clean. I get you're the one who sees her at work. But we still don't know what the fuck is happening at that club and we don't know who's involved and who is there to have a good time. The only thing we know is if something illegal is happening, it's not out in the open. But that doesn't negate the fact it still might be happening, and Sloane Ellis might not be who you think she is. But right now, I'm not thinking about the case or the shit we don't know about. I'm thinking about you and how deep you are with her and why that is. I'm offering you an out. If you need it, take it. If you got your shit squared away, then continue."

Unsurprisingly, Cole had paid attention. Either that or I was seriously off my game.

"I'm squared away," I semi-lied.

"You're not, Ash." Again, it didn't surprise me that Cole called me on my shit. "But I got your back with that, too."

He would have my back. That was Cole—loyal to the end. A man who'd never desert a friend even if he disagreed with him.

I didn't bother denying I was drowning. I'd argue I wouldn't need him to watch my back while I tried to keep my head above the murky waters I'd found myself in.

The truth was, I needed Cole to keep me from fucking up the investigation.

"Appreciate it."

"Anytime. You know that."

I did and he knew I did, so there was nothing to say to that.

4

AGREEING to have dinner with Adam might've been the second stupidest thing I've ever done in my life. Thinking I could find Elise was the absolute stupidest. I was getting nowhere. I had nothing. And every time I went to work, I felt a little more of my soul being chipped away because it meant it was another day my friend was missing. But sitting across from Adam, alone without work between us, was going to not only be difficult—it was going to be dangerous.

I had a new plan. It hatched as I was trying to come up with the words to reject Adam's offer to help plan a party. It wasn't the work that was the problem, it was spending time with a man who I'd come to the conclusion I hated. It was wholly irrational and dramatic. I didn't truly hate the man— I hated that I was attracted to him. I hated that on more than one occasion I'd caught Adam staring at me with blatant interest. But mostly I hated the times he caught me staring at him as he made his way to one of the viewing rooms, and his face gentled and his eyes held what looked like an apology. Of course, I was probably seeing what I wanted to see but I still hated it.

But after I'd tapped out three different versions of a rejection text and deleted all of them I started to wonder if Adam was the answer. If he could be my ticket to finding Elise. I'd hit a dead end. And even though Adam was not a member of the club when Elise disappeared, he was a member now. He might know something. He might've been invited to a soiree I didn't know about.

Maybe the club's owner, Marco Kelly, had a secret coordinator that catered to higher-level members. Maybe there was a membership I was unaware of. Maybe Adam was one of those members and if I could charm him, I could get access. If not to secret parties, at least to his home. I could win his trust and negotiate my way into his bed.

That was my new plan.

I didn't have it all worked out, but I was good on the fly. I'd figure it out. The only hiccup would be the public sex but thankfully it didn't appear Adam liked to engage—sexually, that was. He liked to watch, not indulge in the act.

I could do that.

Maybe.

I could finagle my way into his bed and convince him I liked to watch, too. We could watch together.

My stomach started to get queasy at the thought and it was at that inopportune moment while I was second-guessing my plan that Adam walked into the restaurant and stole my breath.

From my seat at the bar, I watched him approach the hostess stand. I watched his mouth open, his perfect lips form words I couldn't hear, then my gaze went to the pretty young hostess. I instantly wanted to claw her eyes out. Unwelcomed and unwarranted jealousy reared itself nauseatingly fast. My hand shot out to the edge of the bar for no other reason than to keep my ass on the stool, which served as a good reminder I was way too possessive to ever belong to a sex club. But Adam would never be mine, he'd be a means to an end. There would never be anything to be possessive of. Yet I still wanted to shove my way through the crush of patrons waiting for their tables to be called and do something ridiculous like stake my claim.

It would seem luck was on my side—before I could embarrass myself Adam's gaze skidded through the crowd until it landed on me. Without a backward glance at the very beautiful hostess, Adam started in my direction. Perhaps it was his height, maybe it was the badass aura he gave off, or it could've all been my crazy imagination, but the crush of people seemed to part as he made his way into the bar area. He crossed the room with his eyes attached to mine. He looked like a well-groomed, finely dressed hunter stalking his prey.

In an alternate universe, the one where Elise was home safe and happy, and Adam didn't belong to a sex club, he wouldn't need to hunt me. He wouldn't need to stalk or steal or loot. I would happily, gladly, gleefully throw myself at him. I'd greedily take that hungry look in Adam's stare and covet it.

"Sloane."

Silky smooth.

"Adam."

My greeting was met with a tightening of his strong, square jaw. That was not the first time I'd seen that reaction when I said his name, though it was new. Maybe he was one of those dominant men who liked women to call them by their surname. Or maybe Adam liked his women really submissive and to call him Daddy or Master and he didn't like me calling him by his first name.

Welp, he's shit outta luck if that's the case.

"Sorry to keep you waiting. Traffic was a bitch."

Last time I'd checked my watch it had been twenty after eight. He wasn't late, I was early. I had a thing about punctuality. Actually, it was more like an obsession. I despised being late. I didn't like my time wasted and showed the same respect to those I had appointments with.

"PCH is always jammed," I reminded him.

"Actually, there was an accident on the One-Oh-One."

I almost, kind of, sort of felt a twinge of guilt for having Adam come back to The Valley for dinner. I knew he lived in Malibu and me going to the beach since he'd already been in Encino once today would've been the nice thing to do. When I'd texted him a location to meet, I was at the height of plotting my newest ploy to get information about my friend, a plan that was going to include the hot guy I had a feeling would've been the man of my dreams—voyeurism notwithstanding—if I were at a place in my life where I could dream about a man, even one who was off-limits to me. Which meant I wasn't feeling altruistic. On top of that, I was feeling unusually bitchy, and I wanted a steak. And everyone knew Delmonico's was the best place in Encino to get a steak. Yes, even better than Ruth's Chris. Though we would've needed to go to Woodland Hills to dine there, which would've been ten minutes closer for Adam. However, as noted I was in the midst of plotting and not worried about Adam's drive time.

But since normally I was a nice person—some might even call me kind—I did feel that small twinge of guilt. However, I didn't tell Adam this.

"Anyone hurt?"

"Don't have a police radio in my car or a direct line of communication with dispatch so I can't answer that with authority, but if you're asking if I saw an ambulance or a life flight, the answer to that is no. Though someone's likely mighty pissed their Maserati's on a flatbed smashed to fuck."

I tried not to smile at his comeback which also meant I tried and pretty much failed to ignore I liked his sense of humor.

The bartender picked the perfect time to approach, pulling me out of the beginnings of a mental rant about how stupid I was for thinking I could resist Adam, and that was before I found out he was amusing.

"What can I get you, sir?"

Adam's gaze dropped to the bar and then came back to me in question.

"Harvey Wallbanger," I answered his unspoken query.

"Come again?"

"My drink. Orange juice, vodka, and Galliano. Oh, and cherries and orange slices to garnish."

"You're drinking a Wallbanger?"

My eyes dramatically rolled to the ceiling and when they came back, he was smirking.

No, it wasn't a smirk—it was a sinful, wolfish smile that did what it was meant to do. Which was to make me draw up the mental picture of getting a wall bang. And that was exactly what I was picturing—in vivid technicolor. And in that mental picture Adam's naked, sculpted ass was on full display. As were his shoulders, and his biceps were flexed since his big hands were holding me under the ass as his cock—

"Sloane?"

"Hm?"

"You good, sweetness?"

Yowza.

I felt that "sweetness" in my nipples—and other places

besides if I was being truthful. But I wasn't being honest with myself or Adam and since I was already a big honkin' liar, I continued on down that path and pretended I hadn't felt my pussy contract.

God, this was not going to work.

"Yeah, I'm fine."

"Right."

Another smile. This one was not hungry like a wolf but full of arrogance. He totally knew his silky-smooth voice had caused a mini orgasm. My only hope was that my heated cheeks gave it away and in my stupor, I hadn't moaned.

Suddenly a drink was placed on the bar next to a half-full one and I lost Adam's attention.

"Charge it to the table. The lady's, as well."

"Sure thing." I heard the bartender say.

Before we had a chance to get the uncomfortable idle chitchat that ensues on a first date at the bar while waiting for your name to get called, since no one wants to get into a deep conversation knowing they'll be momentarily interrupted, the Hostess With the Mostest appeared.

Okay, that was catty, but seriously she was beautiful with flawless skin and sparkling eyes, and she'd given Adam a nice, long once-over. And as mentioned, I don't play well with others.

"Your table's ready," she told Adam.

Not me. Not *us*. Adam.

"Sweetness, grab your drink."

The hostess lost some of her spunk and I fought a spiteful smile.

Well, I didn't fight it too hard, so it wasn't full-on-spiteful, but it was mildly spiteful.

I grabbed my drink, slid off the stool, and Adam was

right there. Right. There. In my space. His woodsy cologne that I'd come to think of as his signature scent invaded my senses, which was bad. I was a sucker for smells—the good kinds, that was. And Adam always smelled divine, like whiskey and cedar.

I had yet to recover from that when I felt his hand on my lower back—dangerously low. I felt a tingle shift through me, that was dangerous, too. So very, *very*, very dangerous. But when Adam's head tipped down and his mouth went to my ear things went from dangerous to DEFCON one.

"In case I forget to tell you later, you look beautiful."

His compliment floated through the air, wrapped around me, and I shivered. The DEFCON level rose when I felt the barest hint of his lips brush the shell of my ear as he lifted his head.

The next thing I knew I was being propelled forward, which was a damn good thing because his warm palm on my back, his delicious cedar scent, and the lip touch, my brain scrambled, and that included whatever part of it told my legs to work.

When we got to our table, he motioned for me to slide into the booth so I slid in. Adam moved to the other side and did the same. Without any more saucy smiles, the hostess floated away leaving Adam and me alone.

Alone.

How in the world was I going to get through a night with Adam all to myself?

"Sloane?"

"Hm?"

"Sweetness, look at me."

Okay, he had to stop with the "sweetness" business.

My gaze slowly skidded to his and when my eyes met his something strange happened—strange and weird and it happened with none of his normal self-assured, borderline arrogance. Adam's eyes were filled with remorse, but he was staring at me with those guilt-ridden eyes like he'd never seen me before.

What in the world?

"Adam?"

His jaw didn't clench this time when I called his name.

He outright flinched.

Okay, now, what the hell?

But as quickly as Adam's mood had shifted it swung back, his eyes cleared, and the remnants of guilt smoothed out.

Adam ended the silence. "Been meaning to ask—"

Unfortunately, our waiter stopped at the table and interrupted his question with, "Welcome to Delmonico's..."

I sat quietly half listening to the waiter rattle off the specials I cared nothing about, wondering what Adam had been meaning to ask. I did this staring at Adam thinking it was criminal for a man to look as good as he looked, smell as good as he smelled, move the way he moved, have a smooth, deep voice, phenomenal eyes, great biceps, and big strong hands. He was a seven out of ten and I had no doubt that would ratchet up to a perfect ten out of ten when I added the last points. Of course, those contributions to the scale would only be known to the women who Adam took to his bed. But there was no way a man who looked like Adam looked, carried himself with the self-confidence Adam did, and could smile a smug, knowing smile wasn't sporting the sex trifecta—cock, mouth, and finger expertise that led to multiple orgasms. I had not personally experienced this phenomenon, but Elise had and she'd gone into great detail about the magnificence of a man who had both oral skills and knew how to work his dick. But she'd never had a ten out of ten. At most, she'd had a six, and I'd never had above a four.

Elise.

My heart clenched, reminding me my luck had not changed. I wasn't on a date with a seven out of ten who would later take me back to his place and rock my world, giving me all the goodness I'd never had, making him a ten out of ten. I was having dinner with a man in hopes of seducing him to ascertain his role in a sex club.

I was playing a part.

I needed to remember that Adam Newcomb was not and never would be available to me.

I knew I would fail in that endeavor. I knew I'd lose my heart to him—I knew it the first time I saw him. But I'd gladly wrap it up and hand it over, only to get it back bloodied and broken if it meant finding my friend.

Nothing was more important than Elise.

Not a single thing.

5

SITTING across from Sloane was pure fucking torture. She'd gone from the standoffish and distant woman she normally was at the club to over-the-top flirtatious. This would've irritated me if it wasn't so worrisome. The flirting came across as desperate. It was clear in a way that troubled me she was uncomfortable. This was out of her norm and would be—a woman who was as beautiful and self-assured as Sloane would in no way be desperate. She'd never given me any indication she'd behave in a manner that was not who she was. But the woman sitting across from me was not the Sloane I'd come to know.

And for the first time, I started to doubt my instincts.

It had taken one interaction with Sloane, just one, for me to object to her involvement in anything shady or illegal. It had taken me five visits to the club before I started to question if anything illegal was actually taking place. On the surface, Club Joi was a members-only club that catered to the wealthy—high-society, high-profile members who liked to watch and engage in consensual public sex. It was not a free-for-all orgy. I had not witnessed a single woman or man being forced or coerced into watching or participating. It had been the opposite—consent was needed at every step, even from the members who came to the club together as a couple.

No one touched, no one watched, and no one walked into a viewing room without an expressed desire to participate.

However, that was what Marco Kelly, the owner, would want members to see. I had yet to meet him—the club's manager had done my interview. And even though my membership afforded me an all-access pass to all events, a private Platinum party had not yet come up.

Now with Sloane's about-face, I was seriously skeptical.

A few hours ago, she'd made it clear she didn't date members of the club, and considering I'd seen her aversion to the naked bodies roaming the mansion I believed her. Which meant every flirty come-on was total bullshit.

I fucking hated to think Sloane was a bullshit artist, but the evidence was suggesting that was exactly who she was.

And I was getting ready to call her bluff.

"Sweetness?" I called.

Those pretty eyes lifted, and it felt like a punch to the gut.

Beautiful but wicked.

Fuck.

"Yeah?"

"Earlier when I asked you to dinner you told me you didn't date men from the club."

Sloane shifted uncomfortably and her gaze slid away before I read the change in her expression. But if I had to guess it was repentant and in order to ascertain if I was correct, I needed her eyes back.

"Eyes, Sloane."

At my demand, her gaze snapped to mine and flashed fire.

Oh, yeah, all the alluding, all the banter, all the teasing was bullshit.

"I've never dated a man from the club."

I didn't want to, but I believed her.

"Since that's the case, gotta ask this a different way," I started and swallowed down my disgust. "You said date, not fuck. Wouldn't've brought it up but you're giving me mixed signals and just so we're on the same page I'm asking, if instead of dinner I invited you to my bed would I've gotten a different answer?"

I watched her slowly swallow and her cheeks bloom pink, two conflicting responses that confused the hell out of me.

Which meant I pushed to get a reaction.

"Know employees can and most of them do, but I've never seen you participate. So, I'm thinking you prefer privacy."

"I prefer privacy," she confirmed.

Her verification was wholly unnecessary—the look of relief that passed over her body was clearly visible.

My gut revolted as I set my elbows on the table, leaned over my empty plate, and lied through my fucking teeth, which had never been a problem while I was on a job but right then it felt wrong. "Saying it straight, sweetness, I hope like fuck I'm not misreading the vibe and you're interested in coming home with me."

What I actually hoped was that there was a damn good reason for her personality transplant.

"I want to go home with you," she whispered.

What the fuck?

More conflict.

More uncertainty.

The woman absolutely did not want to go home with me, which would've been a hit to my ego if I wasn't so goddamn pissed she was agreeing to something she clearly had no desire to do.

In an effort to calm my temper I sat back in the booth and took her in. So fucking gorgeous. I knew she was two years younger than me at thirty-eight, but she could easily pass for twenty-one. It was obvious she took care of herself —flawless skin, shiny, artfully highlighted brown hair, manicured nails, toned, lean body. Now that I'd seen her outside the club, I understood Work Sloane was very different from Casual Sloane. Work Sloane was tricked out to the nines— heavy, sultry makeup, sexy cocktail dresses, hair perfectly styled. Casual Sloane was just that—minimal makeup, cute but still sexy sundress, hair loose around her shoulders, and with all of that she was relaxed. Earlier I'd watched her shop, I'd watched her interactions with shop owners, I'd watched her bop in and out of stores and walk down the street smiling, happy, and comfortable.

I much preferred Casual Sloane and I gathered that was the real her. Work Sloane was a front. A total put-on. No part of her enjoyed getting tricked out and going to work in a sex club.

The longer I stared at her, the tighter the knot in my gut got.

All sorts of horrendous scenarios played out in my head but the one that caught, the one that made the most sense was Marco Kelly was using her. I'd seen it before. Sick, twisted assholes using beautiful women to lure men in deeper. To give them a taste of what they could buy. In some ways, human trafficking was similar to drugs. A taste leads to dependency. And once the junkies are hooked they'll do anything for a fix. The sex trade was a slippery slope of depravity. Some men liked going to strip clubs and getting their fill of a beautiful woman dancing in front of them, but they didn't actually want to touch. Some wanted a few hours of wild, uninhibited sex and would happily pay a prostitute and walk away. But there were some deranged, repulsive, sick fucks who wanted to own a toy. It was the third kind that needed to be taken down.

What I could not wrap my head around was Sloane willingly allowing herself to be used as bait. In no universe could I imagine Sloane working girls and sending them out to be sold—not even for the night. And if I was wrong it was time for me to quit Takeback and find a new career.

But something was off.

"Adam?"

Fuck. I hated when she called me that. It sounded all sorts of wrong coming from her.

"Right here, sweetness."

"Are we going back to your place?"

Fucking hell.

In any other situation, Sloane asking me that would've made my cock stir to life. Hell, any other situation, her sitting across from me looking stunning, smiling her sweet smile, acting like she normally acted I would've been fighting a hard-on all damn night. But with the turn of events, Sloane putting herself out there in a way that was so unlike her, and hearing her ask me if we were going back to my place, pissed me right the fuck off.

"No, we're not."

"But I thought—"

I knew what she thought, she'd been working it hard all night showing interest that was not real.

"My place is an hour away and that's if we don't hit traffic. We're goin' to yours."

Panic assailed her face before she poorly attempted to cover it.

And since I was pissed, I pushed again, this time being a dick. Sloane wanted to play this game, we were going to play.

It would be up to her when to call a stop to it.

"Is this going to be a problem for you?"

Sloane shifted in her seat, pushed her mostly empty plate to the side, and rearranged her napkin before she asked, "Is what going to be a problem?"

"This. Me and you. Me having you tonight and showing up at the club tomorrow night. I've taken my time, I've watched, but I haven't played. That's about to change. So, is this going to be a problem? If it is, then it's a no-go for me. I can give *you* private but tomorrow I get a taste for it, it'll be you seeing me fuck someone who is not you. If that's an issue for you, say it now and we get on track to discuss the party I need you to plan and forget this conversation happened."

All of that was a crock of fucking shit. There was zero chance I was fucking anyone from the club privately or publicly—period, full stop. There was zero chance I would fuck Sloane and the next day disrespect her and fuck someone else. And there was zero fucking chance after spending a night with Sloane I'd be capable of looking at another woman. But I had a point to make. More than that, I needed her to back down. I needed to push her until she broke from this character she was playing and could get to the truth.

"I don't play at the club because I work there. But just because you won't get the pleasure of watching someone else fuck me doesn't mean I won't enjoy watching you. So no worries there." After that bag of lies she told, she swallowed hard and continued to bullshit her way through. "The real question is, will it be a problem for you?"

Hell to the motherfucking yes it was going to be a problem for me.

All of it.

Every damn second with Sloane was going to be a problem.

Especially if she didn't drop this act.

I did my best to smile. I had no idea if I pulled it off when what I wanted to do was throw the woman over my shoulder, lock her in a safehouse, and demand she drop the bullshit and tell me the truth.

"No, baby, it won't be a problem for me having you watch me knowing you'll do it wishing like fuck it was you taking my cock."

I'd barely swallowed the bile that pronouncement produced when our waitress stopped at the table. My stomach was still roiling when I handed over my credit card.

And the drive to Sloane's house? I spent that convincing myself if she pushed it I could have sex with her and not hate myself.

6

WHAT WAS THE SAYING?

Fuck around and find out.

Well, I'd fucked around and put my stupid plan into action and now I was going to find out if I could follow through.

Having sex with Adam would not be a hardship if I wasn't lying. Having sex with Adam would be a wild fantasy come to life if he didn't like what he liked. But he'd been clear he had no problem taking me to bed tonight and then having me watch him take another woman tomorrow. That wasn't a wild fantasy, that was hurtful and degrading. That was something in my real life I would never, ever stand for. Not for a millisecond. In my real life, if a man even hinted that he'd get off on something like that I might be compelled to smack him before I walked away.

But I wasn't living in the real world, and this wasn't my real life so I'd played along. It was a miracle I'd gotten the words out. And even though I'd made it clear to Adam I had no problem—which was a lie with a capital L—watching him with another woman, he looked annoyed. I didn't get the look, just like I didn't understand why he didn't like it when I called him Adam.

But I had bigger things to worry about, like how I was going to make it through a night at work seeing Adam with other women. He was nothing to me, but my stupid heart wouldn't get the memo. Each time he showed up at the club my heart cracked a little more. Each night I wondered if that would be the night I saw Adam playing and my heart would break completely. Or if it would be the night I snapped and did something stupid and got fired for tearing an innocent woman's hair out for daring to touch what wasn't mine.

I was seriously fucked. And not in the enjoyable way that left me wrung out and sated. The torturous kind that was sure to leave me bleeding.

Elise.

I had to bury my feelings and stick with the plan.

I had no choice.

I unlocked my front door but before I had a chance to turn the knob Adam's chest was pressed against my back and his mouth was at my ear.

"Last chance, sweetness," he murmured. "You open the door and let me in, your clothes are hitting the floor."

I tightened my hand on the doorknob, my body trembled, my heart wished he'd spoken those words and meant them a different way, my mind scrambled to remember this was about Elise and it was not the making of something that could ever be real.

I turned the knob, the door cracked open, and Adam's hands came to my hips. I thought he was going to push me inside but inside he pulled me back.

"Tonight, you're in control. You don't like something I'm doing you tell me and we'll switch it up. No matter where we're at, you want to stop, you tell me and we stop. You understand?"

Holy shit.

This was happening. I didn't trust my voice, so I nodded.

When I did he went on, "I know the club has rules and you're used to those rules so I'm gonna ask this one time, Sloane, and after that, unless you tell me otherwise I'm taking what I want, how I want it, and I won't be stopping to ask permission. You good with that?"

He was talking about the consent policy.

I nodded again.

"Gave you that once but this is important. I need the words. When that door opens and you step inside, you're mine, Sloane. Every inch of your body's mine. I'm gonna touch you and taste you and fuck you breathless however that comes about. So again, you good with that?"

I wished so badly what he said was real.

But it was make-believe.

It was a lie.

My body would be his for the night then he'd throw it away and tomorrow someone else would be in my place. And I might have to watch.

Elise.

"Yes, Adam, you have my permission."

His fingers dug into my hips, and he gave me a gentle shove and we stepped inside.

The living room was dimly lit by a lamp in the corner. And even though I knew my apartment was just how I'd left it I still glanced around making sure there was nothing out that I didn't want Adam to see. The room was clean and orderly, a sight that always made my heart clench. A reminder Elise was not there to leave something out, or move something, or forget to turn off the TV before she left which she did a lot. Her bedroom was exactly how she'd left it down to the clothes on the floor. I was tidy, she was not. She was too busy living her life to worry about something as silly as picking up clothes. I lived my life but I didn't absorb it like Elise. I didn't have her wild need to experience everything all at once.

"Sloane?" Adam called when I stopped moving. "Which room is yours?"

My apartment was a typical two-bedroom. The front door opened to the living room. To the right was a galley kitchen with a small dining area. On the back wall, behind the dining table, there was a door—Elise's room. To the left, there was a short hall that went to my bedroom. I had an attached bathroom but it also served as a guest bath so there were two doors down the hall.

I tipped my head to the left but Adam didn't move us that way.

"Do you have a roommate?"

Adam's proximity and the heat from his body—not to mention he'd told me he was going to fuck me breathless— my head was fuzzy and my panties were drenched so I answered without thought.

"Yes."

I felt Adam tense behind me which made me tenser since I'd told him something I hadn't intended to share.

"Is your roommate connected to the club?"

Right, the club.

The fucking club would always, *always*, always be between us. But so would all my lies so I guess we were even.

"No."

Another lie.

They just kept piling up. Soon I'd be so deep in them that it would be a wonder if I remembered my name.

"Are you expecting her home anytime soon?"

It was funny Adam assumed my roommate was a woman. I was going to tell another lie and say my roommate was a man just to see how he reacted to that. But there was something in his tone that gave me pause.

"Why? You hoping she'll come home so you can have an audience, or maybe a third?"

The question had barely left my mouth when Adam swung me around and my back was up against the door. All I could see was his angry face and it was coming closer. He finally stopped when we were nose to nose.

"Hear this, Sloane, if I wanted an audience I know where to find it. I thought I made myself clear I understood where you're at. But since I didn't, I'll say it plain—you and me, we don't fuck in public. I don't share what you give me with anyone. Not them watching. Not them joining. And I sure as fuck don't want to watch you with another man or woman. That goes for tonight or any night. So you get a hankering to change up what you've been doing and you want to give one of the playrooms at the club a try you tell me so I can steer clear."

Whoa.

Wait.

What?

"But you said—"

I didn't finish. Not because I didn't have very important topics to cover but because Adam's mouth slammed down on mine and I lost my train of thought. Then his tongue pushed into my mouth, and I was just plain lost. It took less than a second for the kiss to go from something necessary to instigate my plan to the best kiss of my life. It was deep and wet and demanding but still managed to be beautiful. And since I was so far gone in my delusion it felt real.

Me and Adam.

Just the two of us.

Nothing between us.

The kiss was so good my hands went to the back of his neck and laced together. His hands cupped my behind, but they were not still. I could feel the material of my sundress inching up the back of my thighs until he had it bunched up and his palms were on my cheeks.

Nice.

I felt the tips of his fingers skimming the edge of my boy-short undies and I stiffened. Not the sexiest panties—as a matter of fact, it was mortifying. But everyone knew you didn't wear a G-string under a dress unless you didn't care if a gust of wind blew and showed off the goods.

Unfortunately, Adam must've felt the tension because he broke the kiss.

Thankfully, he misread it and suggested, "Your room."

Okay, maybe it wasn't a suggestion as much as it was a command. Adam dropped the hem of my dress, stepped back, nabbed my hand, and dragged me across the living room to the short hall and opened the door to the bathroom. He saw it wasn't my room and tugged me farther until he reached another door and opened the closet.

"Jesus," he grumbled and kept walking.

As they say, the third time was the charm. He pushed open the door and flipped on the light which, thank the good Lord only lit one small bedside lamp with low voltage, not a blinding overhead light that would highlight my every flaw.

Then my dress was gone.

G.O.N.E.

I didn't know how it happened so quickly but the last I saw of it was the pastel yellow fabric sailing through the air before it landed on the carpet. But I didn't get a chance to contemplate how Adam had managed the maneuver, or if I thought it was the hottest thing that had ever happened to me, or if it disturbed me that he was a master, and how many women he had to have practiced that on to get to the level of skill. And I wasn't able to contemplate that because I was on my back on my bed with Adam's mouth between my legs and I was contemplating something new.

My ugly panties were still on, Adam's hot breath filtered by the fabric. The feel of that was somehow naughty. Frustrating but naughty. My hands went to the waistband, Adam's head came up, and my breath froze. The erotic sight of his handsome face between my legs made me dizzy.

So dizzy I stopped pulling at my undies and stared.

"Good girl."

Did he just say that?

And did my sex flutter hearing it?

Yes. Fuck yes, it did.

Not only did it flutter but I'd pretty much do anything to hear him say it again in that sexy gruff tone.

He lowered his head but turned his face and pressed a soft kiss to the inside of my thigh.

"I want you naked," I told him.

He ignored my request and continued to give me lazy kisses down my leg, inching his way toward my center.

I wanted my panties off and his mouth back where it was. I wanted his clothes off so I could see and touch his bare skin and I wanted both of those equally and fervently.

I didn't get what I wanted but that didn't mean my body wasn't vibrating. It didn't mean that every gentle kiss and swipe of his tongue against my sensitive skin didn't make my need grow until I was panting and ready to beg. Finally, his thumb dipped under the gusset of my panties and my back arched off the bed in hopes of getting more. With his lips at the juncture of my hip and thigh, the pad of his thumb skimming my opening I couldn't hold back my moan. But when his thumb slid up and circled my clit I lost whatever control I had left and rocked against his thumb while crying out.

"Adam."

His name seemed to spur him on, and his control slipped too. He surged up and was over me with his mouth back on mine, kissing me hot and heavy. His hand between my legs kept at my clit making magic, building an orgasm. Though I was pretty sure I could've climaxed from the kiss alone. Adam kissed like he carried himself—confident, assured, cocky. He took, he controlled, he demanded, but he gave.

Holy shit did Adam *give*.

And just as I was tipping over the edge his phone rang. *No!*

His thumb pressed deeper, he growled into my mouth, and his hand resting on my hip tightened until his fingertips were digging in to the point of pain.

All of that sent me flying.

He swallowed my groans by deepening the kiss.

The phone stopped ringing right about the time he slowed his thumb and gentled his kiss.

I was ready to get to the good stuff. Not that my climax wasn't sweet but if he could do that with a kiss and some heavy petting, I wanted to see what else he could do. And I wanted my turn.

Adam broke the kiss, shifted to the side, and slid his

hand out of my panties to reposition it, cupping me over the fabric.

"Fuck, that sounded good, sweetness."

"It felt good."

He had not changed clothes from when I saw him on the street and for some reason that thrilled me. Only Adam could get away with going to a semi-fancy restaurant in jeans and a tee. But since he was still wearing the same t-shirt I now got to live out my earlier fantasy and take it off of him. With that in mind, my hands went to the back of his shirt and I started to pull it up.

His phone rang again.

A look of relief mixed with frustration passed over his face.

Not good.

Adam dipped his head and touched his lips to mine before he rolled to the side and fished his phone out of his pocket.

"I need to take this," he told me as he answered the call. "Yeah?" There was a beat of silence before his face turned to stone and his eyes went to the pillow under my head. "Right. I'm in The Valley. I'll be there in an hour."

He disconnected the call. His eyes came back to me and they warmed when he gave me the bad news.

"Gotta go, sweetness. Work."

Work?

This late?

I didn't verbalize my thoughts.

I nodded and said, "Okay."

"I wouldn't leave if it wasn't important."

I wanted to believe that with my whole heart but I didn't. I saw his relief that we'd been interrupted. I saw it clear as day and I didn't believe that Adam did anything he didn't want to do. Which meant if he wanted to stay he'd stay and deal with work later.

"Okay," I repeated.

"Dinner at my place tomorrow. We'll go over what I need for the party."

My heart cracked a little more.

The party.

"I work tomorrow night."

For a businessman who was as successful as he was, he sure did suck at hiding his emotions. The relief and frustration had vanished, and straight-up anger suffused his features.

"I know our night's cut short, but I meant what I said earlier."

He'd said a lot of stuff. Some of it sexy, some of it scary, and some of it confusing.

"You don't strike me as a man who says things he doesn't mean but I need you to be a little more specific."

Adam tossed his phone on my bed and as soon as his hand was free it moved to the side of my neck and settled there. His fingers lightly skimmed the area under my ear as he spoke.

"Meant what I said about not wanting to watch you at the club."

I immediately stiffened, not sure if I was pleased that he didn't want to see me with another man or seriously pissed he was one of those control-freak assholes who did whatever they wanted, including screwing other women while they demanded loyalty from their partner.

"You don't get to make that demand," I snapped. "I told you I don't date men who belong to the club, and I meant that. I'm also not the kind of woman who allows a man to boss her around."

The tips of his fingers dug into the back of my neck and his face dipped closer. Once he had all of my attention he went on.

"I do not share what's mine. Period. Not ever. You can lay under me and try to bullshit but I know you feel it the same as me. I know it started for you the first time you saw me. I know it because you didn't hide your disappointment seeing me at the club. At the time I didn't get it, now I do. It started for me at the second party I went to, and I saw you in that red dress."

I knew the red dress Adam was talking about; it was the only one I owned. Red wasn't my color but when I found an Alexander McQueen in a consignment store in Thousand Oaks, I couldn't pass it up. The dress fell mid-thigh, only gave away a hint of cleavage, and was tight but not so tight I had to suck in my stomach all night or wear a pair of those annoying tummy shapers, making the dress sexy without being trashy.

I loved that he remembered the dress, but I didn't love where this conversation was headed.

"I'm not yours," I rebuffed. "I won't *bullshit* you and deny I was disappointed you're a member. Given our current position, obviously, I find you attractive. But my rules are my rules, and I don't date members and I do not share, ever."

"But you'll fuck them," he rasped then added, "in private."

His accusation tore through me, ripping me to shreds.

I was all for women getting what was theirs however they wanted to get it. The old and tired double standard was just that—tired and old. Men who played the field and had sex with whomever they wanted had always been a-okay but when a woman enjoyed sex however that came about, she was looked upon poorly.

Fuck that.

Women liked good sex just as much as men and I suspected women really liked great sex. Unfortunately, in my limited experience, I'd only had mediocre to good sex but that didn't mean I wasn't on the lookout for the elusive ten out of ten and I felt no shame in that.

But the way Adam had spat the words made me feel...*icky.*

Elise, I reminded myself.

"Who I fuck is none of your business, just like who you fuck is none of mine. Now, since we're done here, get off me."

He didn't get off me, oh no, his eyes narrowed and he stayed right where he was.

I'd seen enough of those crime shows to know I should've been worried I had an angry man pinning me to the bed. I didn't know Adam from well...Adam, but for some reason, I knew he wouldn't hurt me. Not physically.

I bet all the dead-in-a-ditch women thought the same thing before they were strangled to death.

"I'm not leaving until you tell me you understand me. Until this is done, you're mine. Again, I do not share. You want the same from me, you got it. So we're clear on that, while I'm at the club I will not touch or be touched—that's yours and only yours."

But he'd watch.

If I was reading this right, he'd still go to Club Joi, sit back in a viewing room, watch all sorts of sex play out in front of him, get turned on, then he'd fuck me in private.

He'd get his kink and get off.

Ugh.

Every ounce of my self-respect screamed at me to tell him to go fuck himself. It was all or nothing. Me or the club. I would not and could not be the sex toy that was nothing more than a glorified receptacle.

That was gross.

Disgusting, even.

But for my plan to work I had to play the part. I had to swallow my pride and dignity and get what I could from Adam. He was nothing more than a pawn.

I'd never be his.

The thought shouldn't have crushed me—evidence suggested he was a total douchebag—but it still did.

"Fine. No touching or being touched. But only if you promise I get no problems from you while I'm at work. I have a job to do, and I can't have anything fucking that up."

Those already narrowed eyes turned to slits before he cleared his expression.

"Tomorrow night, my house, six. I'll text you the address."

"I have to be at work at eight."

"And?"

"That only gives you two hours."

A devilish smile tugged at his lips, making my already wet panties wetter.

"Sweetness, if you're worried about me having time to get you off, don't. You get that hot for me from a kiss I can't wait to watch you come apart when I get my mouth on that sweet pussy."

I wanted to remind him it wasn't all from the kiss but it mostly was. He was fantastic with his mouth so I was pretty sure with it between my legs I'd have an out-of-body experience, and since I wasn't living life in the real world but in this dark and murky underworld, I was going to take every pleasure I could from Adam without feeling a morsel of degradation.

I was aiming for nonchalance, but I was pretty sure I was panting when I said, "We'll see."

"Yeah, baby, we will. We're also gonna hear you chantin' my name when you come on my tongue."

"Just on your tongue?" I teased. "No other parts of you are gonna make me—"

My words died when Adam flexed his hips and I felt the hard length of him press against my inner thigh.

"Just my tongue. By the time I give you my cock you'll be incapable of speech."

With that, Adam pressed a kiss on my forehead, moved down to press another on my throat, then continued farther, and feather-light dragged his tongue down between my bra-clad boobs. He didn't go for more, just that, a tease of his tongue.

"Gotta roll out, Sloane, but I'll see you tomorrow."

And with that, he nabbed his phone and rolled.

Off the bed, then out the door.

I lay there unsure how I felt about this. He didn't pause to take in my mostly naked body. He didn't ogle me, even though he could've. He didn't look back, he just left.

Part of me was disappointed—the other part was wondering what the fuck was wrong with me.

Holy shit, that just happened.

Okay, this was good.

Adam took the bait.

I could do this.

I had until tomorrow at six to get my head on straight.

I was getting closer, I could feel it.

Maybe Adam was the key to unlocking Club Joi.

7

"YOU WANT to talk about it yet?" Cole asked.

No, I didn't want to talk. I swallowed the last of my beer and set the empty bottle on the deck next to my feet, but kept my eyes aimed at the surf.

I was a motherfucking scumbag.

No two ways about it.

I spent the drive back to the beach alternating between being pissed as all-fuck at Sloane for opening her damn door and stepping inside, and at myself for being a weak douchebag. Thank fuck Wilson called when he did to tell me he was in town.

It was only by some sort of divine strength of will I'd managed to keep a minuscule hold on my control, but when I got my hand in those ridiculous panties and I felt how fucking wet Sloane was, that control I'd been holding onto nearly snapped. When she came apart my determination to not take it beyond where we'd gone only held because I couldn't stop hearing her call me Adam. Me fingering her to orgasm might've been an asshole thing to do, but at least I'd kept my dick in check.

Which meant tomorrow was going to be tricky.

I figured she'd cave, especially when I declared Club Joi off-limits to her, agreed not to sexually participate, but alluded to still watching. Sloane had never struck me as the type of woman who would allow herself to be disrespected. And it was only disrespect because it was blindingly clear she didn't get off on any of the club's offerings. I saw her anger flare but she hadn't called me out on it. Which shocked the hell out of me and disappointed me in equal measure. I'd fully expected her to at the very least call me out and make watching a hard limit for her. But she didn't, she fucking agreed.

She'd started the game and now she was going to play it out to the bitter end even if that meant having sex with me.

What in the hell would drive a woman who was as self-possessed as Sloane to fuck a man who was into a kink she found objectionable?

She was as attracted to me as I was to her, no doubt. But attraction only goes so far when the object of your attraction is an asshole.

Sloane Ellis would not put up with an asshole.

"We're missing something," I told Cole. "This shit with Sloane tonight was not right."

"You didn't take advantage of her," he carefully stated. "You said you were clear about what was going to happen."

I could swear I felt a filling in my molar pop free with the amount of pressure I was using to clench my jaw.

There were a lot of fucked-up things about my night—having to tell Cole the specifics of it was damn near the top. It felt like a betrayal to Sloane. It felt like something some meathead dickwad would do while sitting around with his buddies, drinking beer, bragging about pussy. Not that I was bragging, and I left out bringing her to climax, but I did need to report I had her out of her dress and on her bed.

Fucked-up shit!

"I made it clear, twice. She still opened the door. This after dancing around me for two months, being shy and cautious, trying hard to hide she's into me even though she really doesn't want to be. After she turned me down flat to dinner when she thought it was a date. Then out of the blue, she starts flirting. I was not cool about it when I asked her if she fucked members; the Sloane I thought I knew would've slapped the hell out of me for being a dick. Then she straight-up says she wants to go home with me, knowing the implication is I want to take her there to fuck her. I'm telling you, that is not the Sloane I know. We are missing something. Something has that woman tweaked."

"Two things," Cole started. "Maybe she decided to act on whatever's been brewing between the two of you. Believe it or not some women like meaningless sex." I shot Cole a middle finger for being a condescending prick. Undeterred he went on, "Or she's got her orders to feel you out before Kelly offers you more than your membership at Joi outlines in the fine print."

"Ten minutes into my dinner with her, I questioned her innocence. I started to doubt myself and my instincts," I admitted. "But you did not see her, she was conflicted. I think the only honest thing she said tonight was that she didn't share and she wouldn't be shared or watched. It's fucked-up and I cannot explain it but it's in her eyes. She wants to act on her attraction, but she thinks I'm the asshole I've led her to believe I am. She doesn't want one thing to do with that club, not one. She does not like being there. She wouldn't be involved with a sex club unless she had to be. Unless someone was holding something over her head. I'm telling you, Cole, and you can think I'm an idiot, but my gut has never led me astray—there is something wrong. I can't get a read on the club. It's on the up and up, all of it. Not even a whiff that something shady's going on. At least not until Sloane turned. Now I'm wondering who's forcing her to get me on the hook."

"I'll dig deeper into her life," Cole conceded. "But, Asher, you need to be prepared to be pulled from this assignment. Wilson's here to tie up loose ends and punt the report to the SOIB. Our part's almost done."

Fuck.

"She has a roommate. I didn't see that on the original report, but she mentioned it tonight. I asked her if she was a member of the club. She said no, but the way she stiffened in my arms I'm not sure I believe that."

"There's no roommate on the lease," Cole confirmed. "I'll start there and check the parents, see if they've recently come into debt or illness, something that would tip Sloane into doing something out of the norm with the promise of helping her family out of a tight spot."

Now that I could see Sloane doing.

That was the type of woman I believed her to be.

"Any word from Wilson?"

"Yeah, he called right before you walked in the door bitching about an accident on the four-oh-five."

There was a lot to be said about California, but the bumper-to-bumper day-and-night traffic negated all the beautiful offerings of The Golden State.

"Then I have time to shower before he gets here."

"You have time to shit, shower, *and* shave."

I nabbed my beer before I stood to go wash away my shame.

Cole could say what he wanted to try to make me feel

better. And he was right—I was explicit about my intentions, but I still pressed my advantage. I let my attraction to Sloane blur my principles.

I was not the type of man who needed to press advantages. I didn't coax or lie my way into a woman's bed.

Not fucking ever.

The woman didn't know my real name.

And that shit was jacked.

8

I WAS SWEATING in all the wrong places.

Going to a man's house who had been clear his face was going to be between your legs was akin to going to the gynecologist. Every woman knew it was morally imperative to shower before their appointment. *Right before.* Every woman had the timing of this shower down to a science. We knew exactly how long it took us to get ready after said shower, the drive to the office, the length of time it took from our car to the front door. We planned this event to the nth degree.

I had done exactly that. I'd planned down to the minute from the shower to Adam's front door.

But now I was sweating. Boob sweat, fine. Armpit sweat, gross but they make deodorant for that. Sweat down *there* was an immediate stop to all activities.

I was less than three minutes from Adam's driveway.

In three minutes, I would pull up and Adam would meet me at the door. I would not have to knock, he'd be waiting for me. I was certain about this, I didn't know how I knew—I just did. And the insides of my thighs were like a

Montana river after the snowmelt—okay, that was an over-dramatized depiction of the sweat gathering under my skirt, but when a man promised a tongue lashing even a drop of sweat was too much.

I should turn around and go to work early.

I should call Adam and tell him that the champagne wasn't delivered, or better yet the mansion was on fire, and I was needed to help battle the blaze. No, a man like Adam would offer to help extinguish a wildfire.

Damn.

This was a horrible idea.

From start to finish my plan sucked.

Last night I lay awake half the night berating myself for being one of those dumb twits who gets lost in a man's sexiness and overlooks every warning sign he's a dick. It sucked to admit it but that was what happened. I let Adam into my apartment as step one to instigate my plan but the moment he kissed me it was no longer about Elise or finding information that would help me find out what happened to her. It was about Adam.

The turnoff to Adam's private road was right there.

I knew I should've kept going right on past it but I also knew I wasn't going to.

What was wrong with me getting a few orgasms while in pursuit of justice?

I knew the answer to that, so I didn't bother answering myself as I turned down the small road Adam lived on. Each house I passed was more beautiful than the last and they were all gorgeous, prime Broad Beach real estate. The monthly mortgages had to be close to what I made in six months working at the club and I made a decent living.

I found Adam's address and pulled into his short drive-way. I squinted at the two cars parked in front of the garage, one was Adam's black BMW the other a silver Mercedes I'd never seen him drive.

My eyes went from the cars to the quaint porch and there he was just like I knew he would be. I took a moment to take him in, which was a bad idea. Adam in a suit was devastating, Adam dressed casually made him more approachable. Suit Adam I wanted to slowly undress. Casual Adam I wanted to savagely rip his clothes off.

Down, girl, your thighs are already in need of a swamp cooler or an ice pack.

With effort, I tore my eyes away from Adam and reached into the back seat to grab my purse while hoping he stocked washcloths in the guest bathrooms since I needed a whore's bath before any fun times could commence—so I wasn't paying attention, therefore I missed his approach.

But I did not miss his silky-smooth voice wrapping around me.

"Have any trouble finding me?"

Damn, he had a great voice.

"Not to point out the obvious, but I'm here, also I'm on time, so no, I didn't have any trouble finding it."

I figured Adam's silence had to do with my smart-ass comeback not deserving a comment in return but when I straightened in my seat and looked up, I saw him smiling down at me. And by down I meant down—his forearms were resting on the jamb of my car door, and he was leaning forward. His body was shaking with contained laughter and his eyes were doing this sexy roaming over my face.

Why do all the hot men have to be deviant assholes?

In a perfect world, Adam would be a firefighter. He'd rescue cats out of trees and help old ladies across the street. He'd be a hot guy hero. He'd be sweet, but not in a pushover sort of way. He'd be protective and possessive. He'd be a gentleman until we hit the sheets then he'd be demanding and generous.

"Sweetness?"

God, he had to stop that.

But stupid me didn't tell him that.

"Yeah?"

"You keep staring at me like that, we might not make it inside."

I continued to stare, wishing he was real—wishing he was not who he was but instead the man I wished him to be. The man I dreamed my whole life I'd have. The kind of man who couldn't wait to pull me into his arms and kiss me breathless. But more, he wouldn't hide it—he'd tell me straight-out, and by doing so make me feel wanted, sexy, loved.

I was beginning to understand that kind of man was not real. He was the fabled male spawned by past generations of women who'd passed down the lore of greatness from grandmother to mother to daughter, making us believe that one day we'd find him.

"Sloane, baby, you good?"

Baby.

Sweetness.

I didn't know which one I liked better, but I did know I needed to get my shit together. The good news was my nerves were no longer producing copious amounts of sweat now that my heart was pounding in my chest.

"I'm fine. But I'd be better if you backed up so I could get out of my car. Unless you plan on conducting our meeting in my—"

"Our *meeting*?" he cut me off asking.

Lascivious. That was the only way to define this new smile and suddenly I was no longer worried about the mountain stream of perspiration I had going on—I now had a cascade of wetness flooding my panties like the River Nile.

Jeez.

"That's why I am here. We have a party to plan."

That was a load of shit and I knew it.

"Right." Adam straightened while his lips twitched, and he lowered his hand in an offering. "Let's get inside."

I contemplated how rude it would be to ignore this gentlemanly gesture and get out of the car without taking his outstretched hand. Then I wondered why I cared if it was rude or not, we were playing a game of make-believe. The courteous offer was probably part of the act to lure women into letting their guard down. As fast as that nasty thought entered my mind it was met with rebellion. Adam didn't need to lure women into doing anything.

I took his hand, ignored the spark of excitement, and allowed him to help me out of the car. I was faced with a new dilemma—what now? Did I keep ahold of his hand? Did I pull away? Did I kiss him? Did I play hard-to-get? Did I wise up and admit I was in over my head and my plan was going to fail?

I heard my car door slam. The sound felt like one of those paradoxical moments in life—a door closing so another one could open. Or was that the final door of my old life closing, trapping me in a world I didn't want to be a part of?

Was I really going to sleep with a man for information? Albeit he was an extremely hot man I wanted to sleep with, but not this way, not for information, not while I was lying to him, and not when it meant I had to compromise who I was.

These were my thoughts as I walked hand-in-hand with

Adam to the front door. Incidentally, I didn't have to decide whether or not I was going to hold his hand—he made that decision when he wrapped his fingers around mine and didn't let go. I'd be lying if I said I didn't like that—both him making the decision to hold my hand, and the way it felt to hold his.

Since I hadn't had a thought in the last twelve hours that didn't revolve around Adam, I'd spent some time wondering what it was about him that appealed to me. What was it that drew me to him like I'd never been drawn to a man before? I couldn't come up with a single reason beyond that it was instinctual. A visceral reaction. I saw him and there was this awareness that came over me, a nagging demand that came from deep inside of me to go to him. It was insane. It made me sound like a fruit loop. But the feeling was real and each time I saw him the nagging became harder and harder to ignore. If I believed in love at first sight, I'd say that was what happened. If I believed in soulmates, I'd say Adam was put on this earth for me.

But I didn't believe in that kind of stuff and further, there was no way God would be cruel enough to make me have to compromise who I was to have him.

But then I had my doubts if Adam even liked being a part of the scene. He'd been at Club Joi for months and no one, not a single new member since I'd started working there waited to get down and dirty. That was why they were there. That was why they paid the astronomical fees. But not Adam. Which made me wonder if this was the first club of its sort he'd been to. Maybe he was just curious if that sort of thing did it for him.

I do not share what's mine. Period. Not ever.

Would a man who belonged to a kink club say that?

Would he readily agree not to participate himself if he needed the kink to get off?

Yep, my plan was going to fail because I didn't know what the hell I was doing. It was going to fail because I was making excuses for Adam so I wouldn't feel yucky about sleeping with him. And it was going to fail because I was going to fall in love with him despite telling myself not to.

I was screwed.

We were through the front door when my head came up. I didn't take in the beautiful view of the Pacific Ocean, clear and unobstructed through the wall of windows. I didn't admire the open floorplan and understated furniture in the room. Nope, I saw none of that because all of my focus was on the two men standing before me.

Two men.

I'd come to Adam's place with the promise of pussy eating and screaming orgasms and there were two extra men in the house.

How could I be so stupid?

Fear and anger swirled together until they were one big ball of energy that infused my blood. My feet refused to take another step, necessitating Adam to stop with me.

Adam lied. He was a fucking liar.

"Sweetness—"

My head snapped, my gaze sliced to Adam, and I skewered him with a look that unmistakably communicated, *go fuck yourself if you think I'm fucking you in front of these men.* Or alternately *go fuck yourself if you think I'm fucking them while you watch, you sick motherfucker.*

Clearly, Adam misinterpreted my unmistakable silent message.

I knew because the bastard smiled.

"Adam."

I got no more out before Adam let go of my hand and stepped in front of me blocking my view of the men.

His smile had faded, and his brows were pinched when he snapped, "Seriously?"

"Seriously, what?" I snapped right back.

Then Adam's face took on a scary look—scary gentle, scary soft, with a big, heaping side of sweet that made my belly flutter.

"Baby, I told you I do not share what's mine," he murmured softly.

See! That right there made no sense—none whatsoever. Why would someone who didn't share pay outrageously expensive membership fees to join a club that was famous for swinging? Of course, there were couples who attended that didn't share. Some of the twosomes came to watch, some came to be watched, but the vast majority took part in all aspects of the club.

Maybe Adam was in the minority, and he just liked to watch when he was unattached, but if he found a woman who interested him he'd leave the club behind.

And maybe I was being a stupid twit who was making up excuses and justifying my crazy fascination with him.

Adam was still Adam.

I was playing him for information, and I should've been grateful that while I was enacting my plan, I wouldn't have to further humiliate myself. But I wasn't grateful, I was totally dejected and bitter.

"Then who are those men?" I inquired.

"I gotta say it pisses me off you think I'm not only a liar but a motherfucker who would feed you a line of bullshit to get you to my house then ambush you with something you made clear you had no interest in. I get you don't know me very well so I'm gonna lay it out straight and hope that this time you believe me. I have less than zero interest in sharing you with anyone. Whatever we have from here on out is for us and us alone. Period. It's not for the club, it's not for my boss or my coworker to watch. It's not for anyone. I get why you'd jump to that conclusion, but I need you to listen to me, hear what I'm telling you, and let it sink in deep. I'm not who you think I am. I would never put you in a situation that made you uncomfortable."

"You're not who I think you are?"

"No, not if you think I'm a motherfucking, cock sucking dick who'd walk you into my home while I have company and fuck you in front of them."

Oh, well, I had thought that was exactly the kind of man he was.

"So why am I here?"

"We had plans. Unfortunately, parts of those plans changed when my boss showed up but we still need to discuss a party, so we'll do that and postpone the rest."

Right. The party. Shit.

"Now, are you ready to meet my boss and Cameron?"

"Sure."

"Can we do that without you looking at me like you're plotting my murder?"

"Yes, now that you've explained the situation to me, I'll refrain from plotting. Though, I wasn't plotting murder. I was telepathically telling you to go fuck yourself. Obviously, since you didn't understand my message, I need to brush up on my skills."

That made him smile.

"I got the go-fuck-yourself message loud and clear."

"Awesome," I muttered. "Introduce me?"

"Yeah, sweetness, I'll introduce you."

He didn't introduce me, not right away. Not before he

leaned forward and kissed my temple. When he pulled back, he was once again smiling.

"Didn't get a chance to tell you, but you look beautiful."

I wanted to swoon at his compliment. I want to believe that this handsome man was real and this was the beginning of something special. But it wasn't, so I didn't swoon. I braced for the inevitable pain instead.

After that introductions were made, handshakes were given, and pleasantries were exchanged. And since my anger had faded, I took in my surroundings, including the two men. They had the same air about them that Adam had —leaning on the right side of arrogant, meaning they were confident, not egomaniacs. Both of the men were extremely good-looking; tall, broad-shouldered, lean. His boss, Wyatt, had some silver in his hair which in no way deducted from his hotness—it actually ratcheted it up. Cameron looked like the personification of the bad boy who would be oh-so-fun to spend the night with but that was all you'd get with him.

"So, Adam says you're the executive event coordinator for Club Joi," Wyatt said as soon as I took my seat at the table on the back deck.

Here we go.

I waited for the lewd stare or a salacious comment, but surprisingly none came.

"I am. Before that, I worked for one of the largest event production companies in Los Angeles."

"Why the change?" Cameron inquired. "If you don't mind me asking."

I did mind. I didn't want to talk about why I quit my previous job and for obvious reasons, I couldn't tell them the truth.

More lies to remember.

"I just wanted a change. Or perhaps I wanted stability.

With my previous employer I planned an event, executed it, then got a new assignment and started all over. With the club, I still have to plan and execute but without the headache of new clients."

I was looking directly at Cameron so his intense study of me didn't go unnoticed, but it was Wyatt's I sensed. I couldn't see it, but I could feel his penetrating attention, and it scared the crap out of me.

I felt Adam's hand on my bare thigh. I didn't know what I expected, maybe for him to go all Mr. Grey on me, and despite what he said about not sharing me with anyone, slide his hand up and see if he could make me squirm. But his hand didn't move, his thumb did—slowly and gently skimming my leg. The touch was too much to be a friendly gesture, but it wasn't sexual either. It was familiar but calming. And when my gaze shifted to Adam, suddenly I understood all those stares he'd given me over the last few months and why I sought them out. He settled my nerves, he calmed my thoughts, he was my touchstone when I was so far out of my element, I thought I'd go crazy.

It wasn't until Adam joined the club that I felt comfortable there, safe.

Protected.

How weird was that?

I pulled in a breath, shoved aside my terrifying thoughts, and rallied.

"Adam said you're looking for a small meet and greet." I looked around the small deck before my gaze settled on Wyatt. "This place is beautiful, the view is great, but the parking is horrible even for a small party. I have a few connections for venues. We could do Hollywood Hills or if you want the beach, I know a property owner in Malibu."

"Malibu."

"Good choice." I nodded and reached for my tablet in my purse.

Adam gave my leg a squeeze. I ignored the thrill I felt and slipped into my role as an event planner.

And, yes, I did this knowing Adam was sitting next to me offering me more of his comfort, safety, and protection.

The question was, who or what was Adam protecting me from? Something wasn't quite adding up. Something was off. Something that should've made me run from Adam but instead pulled me in.

The answers to those questions came sooner than I thought.

Much sooner.

I'd also learn the door I heard slamming was the door to my old life. It clicked closed and when I tried to reopen it—it was locked.

9

"I'LL DIG DEEPER," Cole told me as soon as I entered the house from walking Sloane to her car.

He'd been in Sloane's presence for two hours, though all it had taken was fifteen minutes for him to see what I saw.

"That'd be good since I thought we agreed to that last night."

"We did, but I wasn't fully committed. Or I should say I wasn't fully sold, now I am."

I wasn't sure if I was pissed or pleased but I didn't get a chance to fully examine my feelings before Wilson walked in from the back, phone to his ear, eyes on me.

"I need that by tonight, Rhode." I heard him say. "Pull in Jack and Davis if you need. Cole's working on the parents now." There was a pause then, "Good. Talk soon."

"That woman's hiding something," Wilson announced.

No shit, I thought.

"Run down the club for me again."

We'd already debriefed last night when Wilson dragged his miserable ass in after a four-hour drive from the airport.

"No signs of prostitution. No drugs. No coercion. No

one underage. Consent is mutual and strictly adhered to. Other than Sloane, everyone who is there wants to be there and enjoys their time there. No rumors. No badmouthing other members. Nothing. If something wasn't going on with Sloane, I'd say the SOIB got it wrong."

"What about the horseback rider who called the police about the underage girl?" Wilson pushed.

The phantom girl was the reason the Marshals decided to look into Club Joi. A man who had been out riding his horse on the state park land that bordered the mansion reported to the police he had seen a woman running near the gate naked. When the man got closer to the fence that surrounds the property the rider said it wasn't a woman, but a young girl and she looked like she'd been whipped. The police who investigated found no signs of the girl but one of the detectives didn't like the vibe of the mansion and took it upon himself on his own time to case the place. That detective broke rank and sent his intel to the Marshal Service hoping they'd do something. Which they did; they contracted Takeback.

"I don't know," I admitted. "I've been to the club every night it's been open and one of us," I tipped my head toward Cole, "has been watching the place the other nights and it's been quiet. No private parties I wasn't invited to. No cars in or out. As for the whipping, I haven't seen anything that hardcore. Spanking is the only impact play I've seen. No humiliation, no rope play, no Dom, sub, or anything that resembles BDSM. That's not their kink. It's vanilla sex with a twist. They like to watch and be watched and some like to share."

"Sounds boring," Wilson mumbled, and I had to choke back my laughter.

Cole didn't bother. He also didn't hold back his

comment, "Damn, boss, good old fashion vanilla not do it for you?"

Wilson ignored the jab and continued, "Lorenzo Kelly?"

The owner's son. One of the reasons Wilson flew from Idaho to California.

"The guy is a grade-A dickbag. I got the feeling no one likes him. I can't say he did anything that would be considered against the rules but everyone at the party gave him a wide berth. He's an entitled prick and doesn't hide the fact he thinks he's above everyone else. His father owns the club so it could be that no one wants to accidentally say or do something to offend him and lose their membership. Or it could be they're trying hard not to punch the asshole in the mouth, so they steered clear to stay out of trouble. I didn't like the way he was eyeing up Sloane, but straight up, I wouldn't like *anyone* eyeing her up. So, if it was just her, I'd cop to being jealous, but he was studying the women, all of them. And no one was getting off on the way he was doing it. It wasn't kink, it was filth."

Wilson's jaw clenched and it didn't relax when he said, "You need to get her to talk. However that comes about. Rhode's trying to find out who the roommate is. If he runs into any problems, he'll call in Shep. But getting ahold of Shep is a pain in the ass and could take a few days. If that happens, I'll sit on Sloane's apartment, get a shot of the roommate, and run it through facial rec. Cole's gonna continue digging into her parents. When he's done with that, he can help Rhode. I have a call into Lorenzo's office asking for a sit-down. If that doesn't get me a face-to-face, we'll send him an invite to this meet-and-greet you're having Sloane plan. Which by the way was a good save but I hope you have the guest list handy or your great idea's gonna blow up in your face."

Pillow talk.

My stomach revolted at the idea.

"We might have to have the rest of the team fly down," I admitted.

"That's a fuck no," Wilson returned. "If Rhode and Reese come down here Brooklyn and Sadie will want to come. And where Brooklyn goes Letty goes. And that, my friend, is where your plan will blow up. Those two will scare the fuck out of Sloane."

Actually, I thought Sloane would get along well with Brooklyn, Letty, and Sadie. If anyone could get her to talk it would be Letty. The woman was pathologically friendly— she was also pushy and nosy.

"Maybe—"

"Fuck no," Wilson cut me off and repeated. "Trust me on this. You want something to come out of this beyond closing a case. You get Sloane to talk."

"Beyond closing a case?"

Wilson practically rolled his eyes before they swung to Cole.

"You know what they say, boss," Cole started. "The course of true love never did run smooth."

"Plato's—"

"Shakespeare," Cole corrected.

"I don't give a shit who said it," Wilson interrupted. "But damn if it isn't true. And if you were trying to hide whatever it is you got going on for Sloane, hate to tell you but you failed. So I'll repeat—get her to talk. The sooner she does, we can clear her, and you'll have a clean go of it."

"What he means is, you can get on your knees and beg

her to forgive you for lying to her about who you are and what you do, Adam."

Fuck.

"It's not like..." I trailed off, unable to finish the lie.

It was *just* like that.

The problem was I wasn't exactly sure what *that* was.

Plus, Cole was right, I'd been lying to Sloane since the day I met her. Then there was the added complication that she lived in California and I lived in Idaho.

I decided it would be best to dodge the topic altogether and employ evasive maneuvers.

"I have to get ready."

"Get her to talk," Wilson repeated as I walked away.

———

SLOANE HAD CHANGED from the sundress she had on earlier into a form-fitting cocktail dress that left nothing to the imagination. Normally I would appreciate both the dress and especially the woman wearing it. But of all nights for her to go out of her norm and wear something revealing was a night Lorenzo Kelly was attending a soiree, his second since I'd been a member. And just like the first time, I didn't like the vibe he gave off or the vibe of the club. The atmosphere changed when he entered a room and it fucking sucked that the first night back at a party after coming to an agreement with Sloane I couldn't hang back in the main room. I had no choice but to make my way in and out of the viewing rooms. And it seriously fucking sucked when Sloane caught sight of me sitting next to the stage watching two women eating—that was eating each other while a man in a mask pounded into one from behind. Not my scene. Not something I wanted to watch most especially up close and personal. But Lorenzo was watching, and not like the others in the room who were obviously getting off on the show. His hand was on his crotch, which was not unusual to witness a man openly adjusting himself, but Lorenzo did it with a glint in his sick-fuck eyes that worried me.

So I was stuck in the room watching after catching Sloane's wounded glare when all I wanted to do was go to her and explain. And I didn't blame her. If the tables were turned, I would've been hurt and pissed that last night she had my tongue in her mouth while she came for me and the next night she was watching a live sex show.

The situation was getting more fucked-up by the minute. And I couldn't stop thinking about what Cole said. Love was out of the question; I barely knew her. But that didn't mean I didn't understand that in a different time and place it could lead to that.

"Unbuckle me, Sherry." I heard the command come from the man sitting to my left.

Fucking hell.

I needed a new job.

One that did not include sitting next to a man getting a blowjob.

Out of the corner of my eye, I caught Lorenzo sliding out of the room.

Thank fuck!

I gave it a few minutes but I was done when the man next to me started groaning. As quietly as I could I stood from my chair, and keeping my gaze averted, exited the room.

As soon as I did my blood pressure went through the roof. Before I could think better of it, I was stalking across the room. Sloane's head turned, her eyes went wide, and her shoulders snapped back. The momentary relief I saw on her beautiful face skated straight to fury.

The woman could be as pissed as she wanted to be but there was no way in fuck I was standing back watching Lorenzo Fucking Kelly lick his lips while his filthy goddamn eyes were glued to her tits.

That would happen when hell froze over.

Sloane rearranged her anger and gave me a tight smile when I stepped close.

"Mr. Newcomb, is there something I can help you with?"

Christ.

Mr. Newcomb.

It would help if she stopped calling me that. It would also help if she found a sweater and coat and hid every luscious curve. Further, it would help a whole fucking lot if she'd open up and tell me the damn truth about why she was working in a sex club.

"Sorry to interrupt," I lied. "There's a spill in the Gold Room."

Or there would be when the blonde on her knees finished off her date.

"Thank you, I'll send someone in." Then she turned to Lorenzo and smiled a sultry, flirtatious smile. "Excuse me, Mr. Kelly."

Sloane turned and Lorenzo's eyes dropped to her ass. My need to rip the asshole's eyes out of his head became overwhelming to the point I was fighting the urge. Thankfully before the last of my control snapped Lorenzo looked over at me.

"How are you enjoying your time at Joi?"

I wasn't.

"Entertaining."

"That's it, entertaining? Are you not finding what you need?"

Oh, I'd found something, I wasn't sure if Sloane was what I needed but I sure as hell wanted her.

I swallowed down the bile and played the part I was sent in to play.

"Yes, Mr. Kelly, entertaining. Unfortunately, your father's club doesn't cater to my needs, yet few clubs do."

Lorenzo's eyes lit.

"Rough?"

"Yes, among other things."

A grin spread across his face that sent a chill down my spine. And seeing as this was not my first rodeo that was saying something.

"I see you haven't used your platinum membership to its full capacity."

"And what capacity is that?"

"Limitless."

Fuck.

"Perhaps I haven't," I started. "But, still, the rules of the club would prevent me from *taking* what I need."

Lorenzo didn't miss my insinuation and his grin turned predatory.

"You misunderstood, Mr. Newcomb. When I said limitless, I meant *limitless.*"

"I enjoy *fresh.* Is that something you could deliver as well?"

The acid in my gut churned but it started to bubble when he nodded.

"So *fresh*, you'll taste nothing but sweetness."

Sweetness.

Good Christ.

"And if I wanted to keep her?"

"Keep her?"

The question was bullshit. The dirty motherfucker knew exactly what I was asking.

"How much extra would that cost?"

Lorenzo waved my inquiry off.

"I don't discuss such things while good times are to be had. We'll meet and plan your private party. Any additional fee can be arranged at that time."

"Looking forward to that meeting, Mr. Kelly. I won't keep you any longer."

I lifted my hand, Lorenzo accepted, and the moment his hand wrapped around mine I regretted it.

Sick fuck.

"Do try to enjoy yourself. All of the women here have some experience under them, meaning they're good with their mouths. At least get yourself a blowjob to hold you over."

With that, the fucker winked before he walked away.

Un-fucking-believable.

I barely contained my disgust as I made my way to the bank of windows that overlooked the expansive backyard. Off in the distance, I could see the fence where the horseback rider had found the young girl. A few hours ago, I'd had my doubts.

Now I had questions.

Was Lorenzo Kelly running a side racket, or was Marco Kelly and the whole club tainted?

I needed to talk to Wilson and Cole. Unfortunately, there were no phones allowed in the mansion.

I had less than an hour until the club closed.

Little did I know an hour and ten minutes later the world under my feet would shift. And when my world rocked my future was cemented.

10

I WAS GOING to have a heart attack. But before that, I was going to crash my car. I was driving way too fast but I needed to get the hell away from Adam.

I enjoy fresh.

At first, I didn't understand what that meant.

Then I did.

And if I wanted to keep her?

Keep her.

I didn't understand that either.

Then I did.

Oh, boy, did I understand that Adam was talking about buying a virgin from Lorenzo.

Gross.

So disgusting, I didn't hear the rest of the conversation because I was afraid I was going to puke on the marble floor, so I tiptoed back to the kitchen.

My plan to seduce Adam was officially over. There was a lot I would do to find information about Elise's disappearance. Having sex with a deranged, repulsive asshole was not one of those things. He wanted to buy a human. A woman. A virgin.

Buy a woman.

I knew. In my heart of hearts, I knew that was what happened to my friend. The police had tried, they'd investigated, but there were no clues. No credit cards used, no money taken out of the bank, her car had been in her space at the apartment, no break-in, no robbery, no calls or texts from her phone which had been in her purse on her bed. Nothing. Just gone. I didn't want to believe it and at first, I held onto hope that she was coming home. But deep down, I knew she was a victim of sex trafficking. I didn't know how I knew but I did.

And Lorenzo. The guy was a creep. He freaked everyone out with his weird stares and the way he licked his lips. But he wasn't around very much, and Elise had never mentioned him to me. Not that she'd ever used members' names. That wasn't allowed; the NDA every member signed protected them from being outed. The club wasn't a secret, and nothing prevented the members who wanted to share that they belonged to such a club from doing so. Elise was one of the members who didn't care, at least she didn't care that I knew. So she shared, but most of it was the fun she was having. How nice everyone was. How much she enjoyed being around people who didn't judge her for liking what she liked.

I was fumbling with my keys in my front door, not remembering how I got home, wondering if I should call the police and tell them what I overheard. I was also thinking about how stupid I was for not hiding a recording device in my bra, when the lock clicked open and I stumbled through. But the door didn't close. I turned to slam it but instead slammed into a wall of muscle.

I knew that smell.

Oh, shit.

"I've been calling you since you left the club," Adam rumbled.

He had—my phone was ringing nonstop since I hit PCH and drove all the way over to Decker.

"I was annoyed you weren't picking up. Then I was pissed when you were speeding over the canyon like a NASCAR driver. Then I was beyond pissed when you hit the freeway and continued to drive like a goddamned maniac. You could've killed yourself, Sloane, what the fuck?"

What the fuck?

What the fuck was—I wanted to get away from *him*.

I didn't say that. I couldn't.

"I wanted to get home. I'm tired. I'll call you tomorrow."

His eyes narrowed, he threw the door closed, and without taking his eyes off of me he locked it.

Fear trickled down my back.

"Seeing as I'm here now, calling you tomorrow is pointless."

Okay. I could do this. I could talk to Adam and when he left, I'd call the police.

"Would you like something to drink?" I idiotically offered.

"What's wrong?"

Everything! I screamed in my head.

Every. Thing. How had I been so dumb? How had I been so wrong about Adam? I kissed him and not because I wanted information but because I wanted to. I'd fallen for him from across the room with one look. And now my stupid heart was breaking even though I was thoroughly disgusted.

"Nothing's wrong. I'm tired."

"Tell me about Elise."

Elise.

I dropped my purse and blinked.

I might've shaken my head, too, but since my head was fuzzy, I wasn't a hundred percent sure.

"Sloane?"

I heard my name, but I was thinking about Adam saying Elise's name. How did know her name? Not in all the months I'd worked at the club had one person uttered her name. No one knew she was my friend. How did he know?

Unless...

My arms came up. Adam's eyes dropped to my outstretched hands, palms out, and he scowled.

Was I next?

"Get away from me."

"Sloane, listen—"

I didn't listen; I turned and ran. This was not smart. Adam caught up to me, twisted me around, and pinned me to the wall.

"Where is she? What'd you do to her?" I shouted.

"Come again?"

"I heard you, Adam!"

I saw the familiar flinch, and seeing that pissed me off.

"God. I should've known."

"Known what?"

"I knew there was something wrong with you. What, am I next? Of course. I'm next. I heard you and Lorenzo talking about you wanting your *fresh* girl."

"Fuck," he snarled. "You didn't hear what you thought you did."

"Bullshit. I heard you ask him if you could keep her. I'm not stupid—I know what that means."

"Baby—"

Six months' worth of pent-up fury unleashed. My first punch to Adam's cheek landed only because he hadn't expected it. My next two were easily deflected. So I switch tactics and bared my nails, wielding them like ten tiny blades. I scratched and fought until I was panting. I belatedly realized fighting was way more strenuous than I thought it would be.

"Are you done?" Adam growled.

With my lungs burning I couldn't answer, thus he mistook my needing a break from kicking his ass for being done. He grabbed my hand and yanked me into my room.

"Now you're gonna listen to me."

"Adam—"

"My goddamn name is *Asher*," he grounded out.

Asher?

"What?"

"My name's not Adam, it's Asher," he repeated.

"Asher?"

"Fuck," he grumbled and tore his hands through his hair. "I'm not here to hurt you."

"You expect me to believe that when I heard you ask Lorenzo for a girl?"

"Sloane, baby, if I wanted to hurt you, I would've already done it. I followed you to ask you about Elise. I had no idea you heard any of that fucked-up conversation with that fuckwad. But since you did, I'll repeat—you did not hear what you thought you heard."

Adam...Asher, whatever his name was, was correct. Lorenzo was a fuckwad.

"Takes one to know one," I spat my immature comeback.

"Seriously, that's all you got?"

"I'm sorry, *Asher*, I don't know exactly what you want me to say. It's not every day I find out I kissed a man who's a vile, filthy pig who likes to fuck virgins. That's gross. But what's worse is I'm so stupid, I was so caught up in you, I was willing to overlook things about you to have you. But this...no fucking way."

"That's a load of crap. You were willing to fuck me for information. You were playing me."

Oh, shit.

"How do you know that?"

"You're not even gonna bother denying it?"

"Why bother? I don't like to lie and you're probably gonna kill me anyway."

"Jesus fuck, I'm not going to kill you."

I wanted to believe so badly. Mostly because I didn't want to die.

"Ask me how I know about Elise?" he demanded.

My heart was already pounding so hard that my chest was burning.

How did he know about her?

"Ask me," he barked.

He was at the club but didn't touch. He watched—not like the others, not with lust, *he watched.* He observed. He never left with anyone. He'd turned down every woman and man who'd asked him to play. He'd watched me closely and called me out on not liking the club, when no one else caught on, just him.

I don't share what's mine. He'd said that to me more than once. He'd demanded that I not participate. He knew I was playing him. He knew at the restaurant, and when he had his chance to have sex with me, he didn't. Even before we got into my apartment, he tried to get me to call it off.

Why?

Then there was Wyatt and Cameron. They'd both watched me to the point they were studying my every move.

"I see you're getting it," he said gently.

"Are you a cop?"

Please say yes.

Please, please, *say yes.*

"No. I work for an organization called Takeback. We work with federal, state, and local law enforcement specializing in the rescue and recovery of human trafficking victims."

The relief I felt shoot through me nearly brought me to my knees. But my reprieve was short-lived. Asher said human trafficking.

"Elise," I whispered. "Do you know what happened to her?"

"I was hoping you could tell me."

"What?"

"Can we maybe go sit down, get a bag of ice for my face, and you can tell me what you're really doing at Club Joi?"

Oh, right, his face. I focused on his left cheek and frowned.

"Shit. You're bleeding. I have a first aid kit."

I was halfway to the bathroom when his voice stopped me and I glanced over my shoulder.

"Sweetness." Asher grimaced after he said the endearment, a scowl so deep he looked like he was going to hurl. "Shit. Sorry. Sloane." He shook his head and then continued. "That's it?"

I guessed since the gig was up I'd get no more of Asher's "sweetnesses".

Why did that hurt so bad?

"What do you mean?"

"What I mean is for the last two-plus hours you thought

I was a sick sonofabitch who was ordering up a virgin. And not even five minutes ago you thought I was here to hurt you and tried to kick my ass. I tell you who I really am, and you believe me?"

Damn.

When he said it like that it made me sound like I was one of those stupid women who investigates a sound in the middle of the night instead of hunkering down and calling 911.

"Yes, I believe you."

"Why?"

I wasn't going to tell him why, it would make me sound nuttier than he already thought I was.

"Because you didn't hit me back when I was kicking your ass."

"Baby, you weren't kicking my ass."

"Says the man with the cut lip and black eye."

I turned and strode into my bathroom to find the medical kit.

I was rooting through the cabinet under the sink when the full brunt of repressed sadness and fear washed over me.

Human trafficking.

My ass hit the floor, my arms curled around my legs, and my chin rested on my knees. Then I lost it.

And that was how Asher found me. On my bathroom floor sobbing like a baby.

But I wasn't there for long. Like some sort of hero, he came in, scooped me off my ass, and carried me to my bed.

Then I did something ridiculously dangerous; I curled into him and cried myself to sleep.

11

I WOKE UP TO A SOFT, warm body draped over me. It had been a long time since I'd woken up in bed next to a woman—both occupants fully dressed, after the woman had cried herself to sleep in my arms, never.

Without disturbing Sloane, I glanced at the alarm clock on her nightstand. Just after nine, meaning she'd been out roughly five hours. That was after she'd burrowed her face into my neck, wrapped her arm around my stomach, hitched her leg over my thigh, and sobbed. Her body shook so violently I'd be shocked if every muscle wasn't sore from the trembling.

So last night we didn't talk. Instead, I did the only thing I could do and held on while tears soaked my skin. After what Sloane had been through, she needed it, and I wondered if at any time in the last six-going-on-seven months since her friend's disappearance if she'd taken any time to look out for herself. Knowing what I knew about Sloane, I doubted it.

Last night when I left the club, I had five texts from Wilson and two from Rhode to call in immediately. After

Wilson briefed me about Elise Keller everything fell into place. I'd been right, Sloane wasn't working at the club because she had some burning desire to organize sex parties. She wasn't there because she got off on the kink and was using her employment to get a membership instead of paying the expensive fee.

She was there to get answers, playing armchair sleuth in a world she knew nothing about. And she'd been damn lucky the club—save Lorenzo Kelly—seemed to be clean or she would've been fucked. And if Marco Kelly found out Sloane had been reporting what she saw and heard at the club to the police, violating her NDA, he'd sue the fuck out of her. If Lorenzo found out, the least of her worries would be shit credit and a judgment against her.

Which brought us to Sloane's about-face. She'd thought I was her in to get deeper into the club. The woman had been so desperate she was willing to fuck me to get what she needed. The confirmation I'd been right about that, too, burned my chest. But the part that pierced my soul was that she thought I was one of them—a sick, twisted, mother-fucker who would order up a woman then hurt her. Yet, that was what my job had been, to convince her and everyone else I was that man.

The hypocrisy wasn't lost on me.

She had no reason to trust me, yet she'd wrapped herself around me and given me her grief. She'd taken my word I was who I said I was. She hadn't asked for proof or called the police to verify—not that they'd have any information on Takeback or our operation but that still would've been the smart thing to do. She hadn't asked questions or drilled me for specifics, she'd simply trusted me. And with the game she'd been playing with the people involved, that wasn't only naïve, that was dangerous as fuck.

The woman was in over her head. It was a miracle she'd pulled off what she had without getting caught.

Sloane stirred and rolled deeper onto my chest. Instead of doing what I should've done, which was wake her up, get her to the beach house so she could be debriefed, I curled my arm around her and enjoyed the feel of her body pressed close. I breathed her in. I memorized the weight of her, the way she felt tucked close, how good she felt there. When I was done committing that to memory, I let my mind wander to the last time I was in her bed. A weird mixture of regret and gratification settled over me. I'd held off and hadn't taken something from Sloane she couldn't get back. I'd held off doing more than what we'd done, knowing I wouldn't be able to look at her or myself the same. It had been the right thing to do, for her and for me, yet I regretted not taking us there. It might've made me a sick and twisted dick but there it was. And as wrong as it was, having her pinning me to the bed, fully clothed, knowing she'd had an emotional night, I was still fighting my dick from getting hard.

I needed to get the hell out of her bed. I needed to get my head on straight and focus on Lorenzo and finding Elise. I needed to stop living in some sort of fantasyland torn from the pages of those romance novels Letty sold in her bookstore.

Too much time with Letty and Brooklyn had fucked with my head. Watching Rhode and Reese find their women, not to mention River Kent swooping in to claim Letty after a decade of being a modern-day version of pen pals, had screwed with my sense of reality.

I was working a case. Sloane Ellis was part of that case and now that I knew her role, I had to put her out of my head and keep my distance. And I needed to do that quickly before it was too late. Before I fell any deeper and couldn't. Before I lost myself completely. After I accomplished that I was cutting off Letty and blocking out her crazy tales of romance.

I hadn't completely formed my plan to extradite my head out of my ass when I felt Sloane grow tense. This became a problem when her hand traveled up my chest and curled around the side of my neck. It became a serious issue when her head tipped back and she pressed a kiss under my jaw.

The issue became more severe when she snuggled closer and whispered, "Thank you."

"Why are you thanking me, baby?"

Fuck.

I had to stop tacking on the "baby".

"For giving me a safe place to let that go. I hadn't realized how scared and alone I felt until I met you. You probably think I'm some dumb, weak woman who's so naïve I'll believe anything and maybe I am. Maybe I'm wrong about you but I don't think I am. Maybe I'm stupid and finding excuses to justify my actions but I've watched you and I knew something wasn't right. Then I came up with some stupid plan to seduce you and you knew what I was doing and didn't take advantage of me even though I was throwing myself at you like a two-bit hooker. So, thank you for that, too."

Jesus. No pretense. No prelude, just straight-out honesty.

It took a moment for me to shake off the shock, it took another moment to battle the new burn she'd ignited. But when I got a lock on that I didn't hesitate to roll Sloane to her back. Our new position was far more intimate—far more dangerous. I planted my elbow on the bed, shifted most of my weight to the side, and used my free hand to capture her face when she tried to look away.

"You're not wrong about me. And since you gave me that, I'll give you this—what you saw at the club was as much as I was willing to give to the investigation. I did not lie when I told you I don't share. To each their own. I don't judge what goes on in that club. At least not what I witnessed. It's just not for me. Not any of it, Sloane. That includes watching. I have a job to do, and I'm committed to carrying that out, however, that will not include me participating. Now you." I paused to make sure I had her complete attention. "Straight up, you working there meant you were part of my investigation. It took me one night watching you to know you didn't want to be there. There's a lot of shady shit I have to do in my line of work; one of the things is not and never will be fucking over a good woman. That includes taking something she's offering under duress. I'm not that man. I saw your play, and you've gotta know the truth; I wanted to take you up on your offer. Not because of the investigation, not for information, because I wanted to fuck you. And you have to understand wanting that had not one thing to do with what I saw at the club. You get what I'm saying?"

"I think so," she murmured wide-eyed.

"You get I'm a man?" I asked and Sloane nodded. "No matter I'm not into that shit for two months, three nights a week I've been watching what's essentially live-action porn. But still, that was not why I had you on this bed with my tongue in your mouth and my hand in your panties. Which, baby, I have to tell you, shocked the shit out of me a woman as sexy as you would be wearing granny panties, especially when you were trying to get yourself some. Though I have to admit, I forgot all about how ugly they were when I felt how wet you were for me."

Sloane's wide eyes turned to slits and her lips formed this half-smirk half-frown that I wouldn't believe was possible to pull off—but more, that it would be cute as fuck if I hadn't seen it myself.

"In my defense, I wasn't sure if I'd be able to initiate my plan. I was on the fence, and I was wearing a dress which meant I needed full-bottom undies. I figured if I got up the nerve to actually flirt with you, we'd make a date and go back to your place. But then you turned all alpha-hero and we ended up back at my place. Then you kissed me and muddled my head and I forgot I was wearing ugly undies until you made my dress magically disappear. But by then it was too late to do anything about it. So you got what you got."

I wanted to laugh at her "alpha-hero" comment but now was not the time to call her out on being cute. It also wasn't the time to be thinking about how well she'd get on with my teammates' women. I could totally picture Sloane sitting in Letty's bookstore, Smutties, curled up in one of the over-stuffed beanbag chairs cackling with Brooklyn and Sadie. Hell, I could see her sitting around *with* my teammates in Rhode's backyard enjoying a beer and laughing at Remy as he ran around being his normal amusing kid self. But that was never going to happen. She had a life in California and mine was in Idaho. As much as I didn't want to think about it, it royally sucked she'd never meet my friends.

I fucking hate I had to ask but I had to.

"Yeah, baby, I got what I got. And since we're here talking about this I have to ask, you okay with what happened?"

A monumental change came over Sloane. I watched it

play out over her features, I felt it sweep through her body, and I heard it hitch in her lungs.

Self-reproach assailed her fast and hard.

"I'm sorry." Her soft apology wafted between us, making my guilt twist in my gut. "I'm really, *really* sorry. You probably won't be able to forgive me for what I did to you, but I hope you understand why. And you have to know that it might've started one way but as soon as you kissed me it became something else."

More truth.

No coaxing.

Damn, she was killing me.

"If you're sorry—which you have nothing to be sorry for —why do you look like..." I trailed off, not knowing what she looked like. There was sadness mixed in there, but I couldn't place the exact emotion that had her forehead wrinkling and her eyes glossy.

"Why do I look like a woman who feels like a—"

Understanding dawned and before she could finish what she was going to call herself I interrupted her. "Nope. Don't say it. And while we're on this topic, let's go back to the beginning. You are not dumb or naïve. For six months, you managed to navigate your way in a world that made you uncomfortable and you held it together. You called it correctly—after watching me at the club you knew there was something strange about me being there. You quit your jobs and went in search of answers about your friend. That's not weak, that's crazy-loyal. And check this, Sloane, I don't care if you played me and five other men and ten women and screwed each of them to get the answers you were after. That still doesn't make you whatever bullshit, filthy name you were gonna call yourself. There are times in life when you gotta do what you gotta do to get a job done. You were doing what you had to do."

"So were you."

"Come again?"

"With me. You were doing what you had to do, but you still asked me if *I* was okay with what happened. But when you asked you looked guilty, like you weren't okay with it."

"Sloane—"

"Don't feel bad about what happened. Please. That would make me feel worse. I started it. I backed you into a corner. I understand that now. My crazy plan to get you into bed put you in a bad place. And that's the only thing I regret about any of it. Can we just forget it happened? Besides, you were Adam then. Now you're Asher. That's your real name, right?"

Yep, she was killing me and I was still on top of her in her bed and she might've been clothed, but she was in a dress that showed a fuck of a lot of cleavage. The dress's length hit mid-thigh when she was standing but was now pulled up, barely covering her panties. As much as I wanted to investigate the cut of those panties I needed to get my mind out of the gutter and get us the hell out of this bed.

"Yeah, Asher's my real name."

I started to roll but was waylaid when Sloane placed her hand on my shoulder and smiled.

"Nice to meet you, Asher."

Fucking hell. I couldn't stop it. I busted out laughing and did it harder when I heard Sloane join in.

Good Lord, this woman was testing every ounce of my good intentions.

"Yeah, Sloane, nice to meet you."

"Is that all settled? Are we good?"

"I'm good if you're good."

"Then we're all good," she confirmed. "Now roll off me, big guy. I need to pee."

I blinked, did it again, and rolled off her while busting a gut laughing.

Sloane slid out of bed and shimmied the hem of her dress down her leg but not before I got a good look at her bare ass cheeks.

Oh, yeah, my good intentions were being stretched to the breaking point.

Time to get a move on it and get out of her apartment.

12

ONE LOOK in the mirror and I wanted to die of embarrassment. Puffy raccoon eyes and night-before makeup were not a good look. At least my hair wasn't a rat's nest, but the smeared mascara and eyeliner around my eyes...that thought morphed into another...a black eye.

Shit.

I forgot about my face, quickly did my business, washed my hands, and flung open the bathroom door. Asher was sitting on the side of the bed, head bent down to his phone, but it came up fast and I saw it—what I'd seen while we were talking. But I'd been so distracted by his big body on top of mine that all of my concentration was going to forming words, so it had escaped me that I'd caused the purple bruising under his eye. Not to mention the tiny cut on the side of his lip.

"Oh my God."

Asher sprung to his feet and in two strides he was in front of me.

"What's wrong?"

I didn't answer him. Instead, I rambled and fought back the tears that were threatening.

"I did that. I'm so sorry! I can't believe I did that to you."

"Did what? I thought we settled—"

"I hit you! You have a black eye."

I watched in horror as Asher's mouth tipped up into a smile.

"I'm sure I don't have a black eye."

"You do. I gave you a black eye!" I continued to screech.

"Baby, calm down. I'm fine. You got one good hit in, which I have to tell you I'm happy you started with the face and not a knee to the nuts."

"Calm down? I punched you in the face."

"You did," he confirmed. "You also thought I was here to hurt you. This after you thought I was ordering up a virgin to deflower. God knows what else was going on in your head at the time. So as pleased as I am I didn't find my balls in my stomach, you ever find yourself in a situation where you feel unsafe, instead of throwing a right hook, you always start with the balls. I don't care if you can't get a knee to them, you grab, squeeze, and twist those fuckers until you feel them pop."

I felt my face screw up in revulsion at his disgusting instructions.

"I'm not grabbing a man's balls and squeezing them until they pop."

"Grab, squeeze, and *twist*," he corrected. "Promise me, Sloane, you find yourself in a situation that makes you uncomfortable you start there, *then* you hit with your right hook."

His eyes held mine and I realized he was serious, he wanted me to promise. As much as I had an aversion to grabbing, squeezing, and especially twisting a man's balls I still found myself giving him what he wanted.

"Fine. I promise if I find myself unsafe, I'll bust a nut."

Wait.

What?

Did I just say that?

Asher smiled hugely at the same time my mouth opened and closed like a fish trying to catch a thought or the right words to correct my stupidity. None came. I was totally speechless.

Asher was not.

Well, he didn't say any actual words, but his laughter did fill my room.

Again.

That was the third time I'd heard him laugh, a sound I could get addicted to. As a matter of fact, I already was.

I also found myself smiling—really, truly smiling—something I hadn't done since the last time I was with Elise. Which felt so wrong but at the same time, oh so right. Elise was still missing, I still had a shit job I hated, and now I knew with certainty that Lorenzo Kelly, my boss's son, wasn't just a sleazebag but the King of All Sleazebags. But for some reason, I felt something settle inside of me. A feeling I didn't want to examine too closely.

"I know we need to talk, and I'd like to hear what you found out about Elise, but before we do that do you mind if I shower? I hate sleeping in makeup and I'm still wearing my clothes from last night. I mean, you are, too, so if you want to—"

"Take a shower," Asher cut off my rambling.

"If you want, after I'm done you can shower, too. You'd have to put back on—"

"Baby, you're killing me," he groaned.

"What? Why?"

He didn't explain. Instead, he bossed, "Take your shower."

"How am I killing you?"

Asher's head tipped up and his eyes went to the ceiling. When they dropped, they were clear of humor.

"Please trust me. Just get in the shower."

"Weirdly, I do trust you," I told him, and his eyes flared. "But I'd still like to understand how I'm killing you."

"Remember what I told you I planned on doing to you during our two hours?"

It took me a moment to remember what he was talking about but when I did my nipples started tingling.

"I remember."

"That wasn't bullshit."

That wasn't bullshit?

"That had not one thing to do with my case. That was me talking to a beautiful woman. Now, do you understand why I'm asking you to hurry up and get in the shower?"

"Kinda," I answered honestly.

I wasn't fully grasping his explanation, but I was fairly certain my confusion was directly linked to the throbbing that was happening between my legs.

Was it possible for a clitoris to throb?

I wouldn't have thought so, but mine definitely was.

Asher groaned and I wasn't sure if it was in frustration at my denseness or if he had some throbbing going on as well.

"How about this?" he started. "From the first time I saw you in one of your pretty dresses, I couldn't stop thinking about getting you out of it. Then when I get my chance, I'm using so much control to do the right thing by you that I don't get to fully enjoy it. But the part I do get to enjoy, got totally fucked when you moaned 'Adam.' Now that I'm standing here without anything fucked-up between us, you're in one of your pretty dresses and I'm using so much control not to rip it off of you and bury my face between your legs, something I've been dying to fucking do for months, it's a wonder I'm able to keep my feet. Please, I'm begging you, go into the bathroom, lock the door, and take a shower."

Hole-lee-shit.

A tremor went through me along with an overwhelming urge to find out if I'd been right about Asher being a ten out of ten. Seeing as just looking at him made the impossible clitoris-throb happen, and his voice made me tingle, I was thinking all it would take would be kissing me again and I'd spontaneously orgasm.

"Asher."

Since he was right in front of me, he didn't have far to go when his arm went around my lower back and his other hand went into my hair, twisting it around his fist until he tipped my head back and his mouth was inches from mine.

I thought he was going to kiss me.

I was ready for him to kiss me.

My body was more than ready to find relief.

None of that happened.

"You get I want to fuck you and I have for a long time?" he asked, and I vigorously nodded not hiding my enthusiasm. "You're hell on a man's resolve."

"I don't under—"

Suddenly, Asher tightened his arm around me and my breath swooshed out.

"Fuck, Sloane, I don't understand either. I just know you're different. Can't say how. Can't say why. I just know you are. Straight up, walking away from you when this is over is gonna hurt like a motherfucker. I take us where I want us to go…" Asher stopped and shook his head. "It'll gut me."

Holy crap, that felt like a sucker punch to my stomach, a velvet blow to my soul. All of it, knowing he felt the exact same way I did—that there was something more, something *different* between us. Something we couldn't pinpoint or understand, just a strange feeling—and both of us knew it was going to hurt not to have it.

It took an extreme, an *insane* amount of effort to step back. But I did. It took more out of me to not ask why— when this felt like a once-in-a-lifetime chance—he would walk away from it, from me, from something that might be. But I did that, too.

I gave him what he wanted, what he'd asked for, and silently walked to the bathroom, locked the door, and took my shower. I let myself mourn our what-could've-been. I did this knowing it was absurd my heart was broken but I did not give a single fuck. I washed my hair, scrubbed my face, and pulled myself together. By the time I rinsed the conditioner out, I'd shoved aside my crazy, ridiculous feelings and refocused on what was important—Elise.

Thankfully Asher was not in my room when I cracked open the door and peeked out. I rushed to get dressed, not bothering with makeup or doing more than running a brush through my wet hair.

I realized my mistake when I walked into the living room and saw Asher standing in my kitchen still in his dress pants and white button-up shirt from last night, looking like his normal handsome self but more so because his clothes were wrinkled and his hair was messy—which looked a lot like how I envisioned his sex hair. I should've taken my time getting ready. I should've come up dressed to the nines, armor securely in place. Instead, I looked like a bum, and he looked hot.

Asher took me in from top to toe and I felt the path his eyes took, up and down twice before his gaze settled on mine.

Ugh.

"Ready?" he asked.

"Ready?"

"We're going out to breakfast."

"What?"

"We are going out to breakfast," he repeated slowly.

"Why are we going out to breakfast?"

"Because you don't have any food and I'm hungry."

"I have plenty of food."

And I did. I'd gone grocery shopping two days ago.

"Okay, I'll amend you don't have anything but yogurt, egg whites, fruit, and some grain shit that looks like cereal, but the bag declares it granola with flaxseed. Oh, and turkey bacon which should be banned or called something else. Poultry and swine are not the same. Bacon is pig. Turkey bacon is an abomination."

Asher stepped into the living giving me a full-length view of his body. I wasn't sure what made me do it; I'd slowly perused his body plenty of times. He'd now lain on top of me twice, which as far as I was concerned, pretty much made me an Asher expert, even if when I'd started my study, I thought his name was Adam.

But bottom line, he was perfect.

"Are you serious?"

"About which part?"

"All of it."

"Yes. We're going to breakfast because your fridge is stocked with healthy crap and turkey bacon."

I didn't know what to say to that.

"How?"

"I'm driving." Again he was talking slowly like I was extra special and the slower he spoke the easier it would be for me to understand.

"No, you jerk. How is it you look like you do and call yogurt, fruit, and granola healthy crap?"

His smile was smug when he asked, "Look like I do?"

"Don't fish for compliments. You know what you look like."

Asher's smile got bigger which felt like a slap in the face, but I'd be damned if I'd let him see the sting.

"Are we going to breakfast or what?" I snapped.

"Waitin' on you."

"I'm ready."

His gaze dropped to my feet.

My bare feet.

Damn.

Wordlessly I turned and tried my best not to stomp. Unfortunately, I think the effort was for naught. I confirmed this when I heard his laughter ring out. Thankfully I was out of his sight when my step faltered and my hand went to my chest to rub away the burn.

I went to my closet and pulled out a pair of Chucks wondering how it was possible to grieve something you never had. I didn't even know the man. I was positive his last name wasn't really Newcomb. I didn't know how old he was, if he was religious or not, if he liked to watch movies or TV or if he read books for pleasure. I didn't know if he had brothers or sisters or if his granny was still alive. I knew nothing. Except when I met him, I felt like my life had been jump-started. When I was in his presence, I felt oddly comfortable, making me wonder if I'd been walking around my whole life on edge. I knew I liked the way he smelled, he was good-looking, and he dressed nice. That was the extent of my knowledge.

Yet I felt him so ingrained in my soul that it was painful to think he'd never be mine.

I grabbed my shoes, shoved my feet into them, fixed the heel, and called myself not-so-nice names for being such an idiot on my trek back into the living room.

I had no idea why I was torturing myself by going to breakfast with him. I could've said no and sent him on his way.

But like the moron I was, I walked to the front door and asked, "Ready?"

Asher's eyes came to mine and that hurt, too. I wanted to know those eyes. I wanted to stare into them while he told me stories about all the crazy things he got up to when he was a kid. And I knew they'd be crazy; a man like Asher wouldn't be boring. I wanted him to hold my hand and smile at me and to make him laugh. I wanted those eyes aimed my way forever.

But that was not mine to have.

And it fucking sucked. However, if he could help me find Elise, I would sit through five hundred torturous breakfasts with him. Later when Elise was home safe and sound we'd open a bottle of wine and she'd listen to my tale of The One Who Got Away. Then she'd jabber on with me about how he wasn't The One and he was really a dick even though we'd both know that was a lie. But that was what friends did, they let you believe the lie until the pain receded and became bearable.

That was my Elise.

I just had to find her.

13

"SERIOUSLY, I want to know how you can eat all that."
Sloane's fork came up and she used it to jab at my plate of
eggs, bacon, hashbrowns, and pancakes. "And if you tell me
you're blessed with a superior metabolism I might stab you
with a butter knife."

I stared at her from across the table and for the twenty-
fifth time since we'd left her apartment, I questioned my
sanity. Wilson and Cole were at the beach house waiting for
us with questions, and while I had some answers there were
more to be had. Yet, I didn't take her straight to the house
like my boss had instructed—I took her to breakfast. Now
that the truth was out, Cole and Wilson would get involved.
I would no longer have Sloane to myself, so I was taking this
time, these last moments of just her and me. It was crazy, it
was stupid, but it was necessary. It wouldn't be long before
the case wrapped up and I'd go home, and she'd stay here.
My time with her was quickly running out—a thought that
made my insides ache.

"There's this place," I started with a smile. "It's called a
gym."

Sloane's brows raised, her eyes widened, she put her forearms on the edge of the table and leaned in deep. "Tell me more about this place," she breathed. Her voice was raspy and full of fake wonder, but it was the way her sexy mouth curved up into a big bright smile that had my dick stirring in my pants. "It's called a *gym* you say?" she finished.

It was then I realized I'd indeed gone insane.

I should've driven Sloane straight to the beach house, or alternately and more satisfyingly, I should've tossed her ass on the bed and done every damn thing I told her I was going to do to her. The truth was out, she knew who I was. The guilt that accompanied the lies was no longer a factor. I wanted her. She wanted me. The end. I could've given us what we both wanted and maybe, *just fucking maybe* my dick wouldn't be rock hard from a smile.

Yet I knew that was bullshit. The way her face was lit and her eyes shining full of humor, it wouldn't have mattered if I fucked her five minutes ago—that smile would still have had me rockin' a hard-on.

"Smartass."

She ignored my comment and her gaze traveled to her plate. After that, she hilariously declared, "Men suck."

"Why's that?"

"There are a variety of reasons, but for the purpose of this conversation, calories."

"Calories?"

"Or more to the point, men's ability to burn them. You see, if a woman ate all of that it would take a five-mile run and a two-mile swim to burn off the pancakes alone. Forget the bacon, that would be another mile of each. But no, not a man. A man walks into a gym and the calories just start melting away."

It seriously sucked on top of everything else wonderful that was Sloane, that I was learning she could be funny.

"I work out to stay in shape, not train for the Olympics. And just to point out, men don't like skinny and pointy."

"Right, so what? You only swim a mile and a half and run two?" she asked, ignoring the rest of what I'd said.

"No swimming." I smiled. "And I was joking—my ass only sees the inside of the gym when there's snow on the ground or it's too hot to run outside and I need a treadmill. Other than that I do my three miles a day outside."

Sloane's brows pinched together and her head tilted to the side when she asked, "Snow? Wait. You don't live here?" Then she added, "In California?"

My identity, employment with Takeback, and the location of the office were not top secret. That didn't mean the company had a website with an About Us or Contact Us page. I hadn't been undercover for an operation since I left the FBI but that didn't mean I had my shit splashed all over the internet. However, I did live in the shadows.

So I had no reason not to answer her question. Yet, I hesitated. Not because I didn't want her to know where I lived but because saying it out loud concreted the distance.

"I live in Idaho."

"You're not walking away, you're leaving."

The sadness I heard in her voice twisted the ball in my stomach tighter. Now, she was getting it. Why I wasn't taking us where I wanted us to go. There was no future and if I couldn't have all of her, I didn't want any of her. A piece wasn't good enough. With Sloane, it was all or nothing.

"What about Elise?" she rushed on.

Selfishly, I didn't want to talk about Elise or the sex club. I wanted to forget why I was in Los Angeles and get to know her better—and that was the crazy part, the part that was totally insane. Now that Lorenzo had given me the opening we'd been waiting for, I'd be gone in two weeks tops. Yet I could not stop myself from self-torture. I had to know what it was about her that drew me in. I had to understand the unexplainable connection I felt the instant I saw her. I needed to make sense of a situation that made absolutely no sense. I'd never in my life felt the pull of a woman so strongly that the thought of never seeing her again made my chest burn.

But I couldn't deny the pleading and worry in Sloane's tone. I had to give her something, even if it wasn't much.

"Wilson already made contact with the local PD and the FBI. We'll see what he gets from them and go from there. If he needs to, he'll reach out to some of our other sources."

"You'll help me?"

Her hopeful stare held mine and it was on the tip of my tongue to make all sorts of wild promises if they'd keep those clouds from returning and dulling her pretty green eyes. But I knew better. Elise had been missing for a long time and the unfortunate truth was, time was not a friend. The longer she was gone the less likely she'd be found alive.

"Of course, we'll help you."

Her relief was immediate and stark. It tidal-waved over Sloane with such force her shoulders jerked back and her neck stiffened right before tears formed.

"Don't cry," I begged.

"So long," she whispered. "She's been gone for so long and I feel like she's nothing but a case number to the police. I know that's not fair but that's what it feels like."

Another unfortunate truth in a city with a population of almost four million and over two thousand missing persons cases on top of all the other crime—the police were spread thin. As were the FBI and the Marshal Service. Reason one to use force multipliers like Takeback.

"That's why you've been working at Club Joi?" I asked even though I knew the answer.

Sloane nodded then followed up with, "I needed to do something."

"Before she went missing had you ever been to the club?" I knew the answer to that, too, yet for some reason, I needed to hear her say it.

"No. She knew it wasn't my scene, so she didn't bother inviting me."

That was an understatement. Looking back at all the times I'd watched Sloane while she worked, the careful way she'd masked her revulsion, I was impressed she'd been able to pull it off for as long as she had. Though the members were there to enjoy themselves and each other I doubted many people actually paid attention to Sloane. Come to think of it, not once had I seen her in a friendly conversation with a member—male or female. I'd never seen her smile, laugh, or joke with a coworker. She was pleasant and professional, but standoffish.

Was that a front, too? Were there more of Elise's friends working in the club and in an effort not to get caught they avoided each other at work?

"What about your friends?" I asked.

"Friends?"

"Did you enlist any of them to work at the club, too?"

She huffed a humorless laugh and sat back.

"No. And when I wouldn't give up looking for Elise our friends stopped calling me."

What the fuck?

"They stopped calling?"

"Yep. At first, everyone was on board to help. They all

took to social media, posting pictures of Elise and asking for help finding her. We decided to go old school and made flyers. They helped staple them to telephone poles, in grocery stores, and dropped them off at bars and restaurants. But then days turned into months, and they said I should get back to my life and leave it to the police. They started calling less and less until finally they just stopped."

I couldn't stop the disgust from bubbling to the surface. *What bitches!*

"They abandoned you?" I spat.

"Not really," she started to defend her shitty friends. "In the beginning, they tried to help. And I don't blame them for backing away. I was working two jobs and when I wasn't working, I was calling the police to see if they'd found something new. And when I wasn't doing that, I was driving around hoping to see her on the street. They warned me I was becoming obsessed. When one of them called all I talked about was Elise. I refused every invitation to go out with them. So they stopped calling. I don't blame them for that either."

Sloane might not blame them but I sure as fuck did. Who the hell abandons a friend? Where the fuck were these bitches' loyalty? Not only to Sloane but to Elise. One of their own was missing and they'd given up finding her after about a month? I would stop at nothing if Wilson, Cole, Rhode, Jack, Davis, Reese, or River went missing. My pursuit would be relentless and unending until I found them, and I knew down to my bones they'd never give up on me either. Same with Letty, Brooklyn, and Sadie—if one of the three of them went missing there'd be no stopping the other two. They'd never abandon each other.

"So when the police weren't getting anything you went undercover and got a job at the club. What were you hoping to find? Did Elise mention someone in particular? Was she seeing someone from the club?"

Sloane's pretty face flashed red, her head dropped, and with that, I lost her eyes.

"I don't know what I thought I'd find," she admitted. "Or how I was going to find it. I was stupid—"

"Hey," I interrupted her. "Look at me, sweetness."

Sweetness.

Fucking shit. As soon as I said the word, Lorenzo's description of his girl came to mind and threatened to choke me.

How many girls did the fucker have? And where was he getting them? Seeing as Elise was in her thirties and a member of the club I couldn't imagine she was a virgin, which made me wonder if Lorenzo had a stable of women or if there was someone else in the club who'd taken a liking to Elise. Or maybe her disappearance had nothing to do with Club Joi and she was snatched off the street—unfortunately, a plausible scenario.

Sloane's gaze slowly lifted. The desperation dancing in her eyes made everything come clear. Why she believed me so quickly when I told her who I really was and why she hadn't questioned me further. Sloane had simply taken my word for it because she was desperate.

Desperate, tired, and out of options.

"You wanting to find your friend is not stupid. You going to great lengths to get information isn't stupid. It wasn't safe but it isn't stupid." I paused to swallow down my thoughts on her bitch ass friends in favor of broaching a more important topic. "You didn't answer—did Elise ever mention anyone at the club who gave her a bad feeling?"

"No. As you know, there's an ironclad NDA. She never mentioned anyone by name and she never said if anyone gave her a bad feeling or was bothering her." Sloane straightened, a new kind of fierceness took over her body language and she leaned in. "Elise is a good person. She likes what she likes. She hates the dating scene. Guy after guy screwing her over, lying about wanting a relationship when really all he wanted was sex. Guys cheating. She'd had enough but she's social, she enjoys sex, she wanted a place where she could be herself and be safe while doing it, so she joined the club."

It was interesting that Sloane spoke about Elise in the present tense. Elise likes, not *liked*. What was not interesting was that she thought I was a dick who'd judge someone for their sexual preferences.

"I think you're aware and understand I don't get off on anything Club Joi offers. But that doesn't mean I pass judgment on those who do. I could give a fuck what consenting adults do. What I care about is exploitation, that's why I'm there. And up until last night, I was struggling to find evidence that the club wasn't exactly what it claimed to be —a safe place for adults to act out their fantasies. So what I'm telling you is, your speech about Elise being a good person was unnecessary. But to add, even if she wasn't a good person, Takeback would still do everything in our power to find her. Now, tell me—have you ever been alone with Lorenzo?"

Sloane's mouth screwed up into a grimace that would've been hilarious if we weren't talking about a fuckwad.

"A few times. He rarely comes to the club."

Before I could continue my questioning, the waitress stopped by our table to refill our coffees, reminding me Sloane hadn't touched her breakfast.

"Eat, baby, we'll finish our discussion later."

She looked like she wanted to argue but instead, she nodded and tucked in.

My morning alone with Sloane hadn't gone as I'd hoped, though it went as it should.

I had no business getting closer to her. It served no purpose.

Some questions were never meant to be answered—it would seem my unexpected connection to a virtual stranger was one of life's mysteries that would go unsolved.

14

I DIDN'T QUESTION Asher when he told me he was taking me to the beach house to talk to Wyatt and Cameron whose real names were Wilson and Cole. I didn't argue when he paid the bill and led me out to his shiny, black BMW, and helped me in. There was very little conversation as he navigated the streets of Encino to the one-oh-one and there was nothing beyond me making fun of him for driving like granny as he drove over Decker Canyon. If he hadn't already told me he wasn't a local his driving would've clued me in.

It wasn't until Asher turned onto PCH that I found my voice.

"I take it this is a rental?"

"The car or the house?"

Right, the oceanfront beach house.

"Both, I suppose."

"I don't know why I bothered to ask for clarification." He chuckled. "They're both rentals and I'll be damn happy to leave them both behind."

His clipped statement was a great reminder he was leaving. I needed to get my head on straight and refocus on Elise. In the months she'd been missing I hadn't had a single moment of distraction—until Asher showed up. Now I was lost in an attraction that would lead nowhere and finding every excuse to defend my lack of attention.

"How old are you?"

Dear Lord, why did I blurt that out?

"Forty."

"Forty?"

"I'm not sure if I should be offended."

"I thought you were younger than me," I admitted.

"Hmm," he hummed. "You sound disappointed. Do I detect a little cougar in you, Miss Ellis?"

I shifted in my seat to get a better look at him. But the moment I caught his beautiful smile in profile I wished I would've continued staring out my window. And when he turned his head to look at me briefly, I really wished I'd kept my trap shut and not asked him his age. That smile was going to be the death of me. It was going to haunt my dreams and break my heart.

"You're joking, right?"

"I don't know, am I? We all have our kinks, nothing to be ashamed of."

I really wanted to know what Asher's kinks were now that I knew I could check public sex, sharing, and voyeurism off his list.

"I don't have a Mommy fetish," I defended.

"A Mommy fetish?"

I shrugged and dragged my eyes back to the side window.

"I don't know. There's such a thing as a Daddy baby girl fetish, I just assumed there was a Mommy one, too."

Asher's soft chuckle filled the car and I fought the need to cover my ears to block out the glorious sound.

"You didn't look at my file?"

I should've been grateful for the change of topic, but I felt disappointed.

Elise.

"I looked at Adam Newcomb's file," I reminded him. "He's a real estate investor with a net worth of twenty million. He owns a BMW and a beach house. He was born in Beverly Hills and graduated from Berkley with a degree in business."

When the silence became uncomfortable, I glanced over at Asher and found his lips pinched together and tipped down.

When he finally spoke, he sounded sheepish and embarrassed.

"Yeah, that was all bullshit. I'm from Wichita, Kansas. I graduated from Wichita State. Before Wilson recruited me to Takeback I worked for the FBI for about thirteen years. I live in North Idaho but that's recent. Before that, Takeback was headquartered in Arizona. I drive a truck and have a small house tucked in the woods. And I'm not worth twenty million, not even fucking close. I have an older brother. He's married, has three kids, and lives in a huge house thirty minutes from my parents."

Holy Christ on a cracker, that was a lot of information. I was a little stunned by his honesty, though I was more curious about the bitterness I heard when he talked about his brother and parents.

"Are you not close to your parents?"

"I talk to one or the other or both of them at least once a week. They use the time as their opportunity to tell me how well my brother's doing. Thriving medical practice, great kids, smart wife, big house on a golf course. It's their passive-aggressive way of reminding me, I, too, could've had a big house and money had I not turned my back on the profession they'd picked for me."

Jeez, his parents sound like real gems.

"What profession did they have picked out for you?"

I was probably pushing my luck but I was desperate to know anything and everything I could about Asher.

"Doctor. My father's a GP and my brother's a pediatrician."

"I can't picture you as a doctor."

"No?"

Once again, his laughter filled the car but this time it was sharp and without humor.

"No. And I can't see you doing something as boring as sitting behind a desk brokering real estate transactions or in a boardroom negotiating land deals."

"What can you see me doing?"

I didn't need to think about my answer, so I didn't. I blurted out my answer instead.

"Something not boring. No suits, no lab coats, no desks. That would be torture for you. Something that challenged your mind but also was physical. You're a natural protector so a cop fits or a firefighter. I could see you working construction or a mechanic or something as equally stereotypically male. Not that there's anything wrong with being a doctor—your father and brother had to have worked hard to earn their medical degrees—but that is *so* not you. And you do not strike me as a man who wants to live on a golf course. A house in the woods fits you, so does the truck. The BMW's nice." I paused to look around the posh leather interior. "But it's too showy and you don't strike me as a man who gives a shit what others think."

The quiet that bathed the interior of the car was a clear sign I shouldn't have let my mouth run away. But the damage was done so I spent the last five minutes of the drive wringing my hands in my lap wondering when I'd become such a presumptuous idiot.

Asher pulled the BMW next to the silver Mercedes, cut the engine, and turned to me.

"When we get in there, they're gonna ask a lot of questions. If you're overwhelmed or need a break, speak up."

Right. Personal Q and A was over and it was back to business.

The disappointment I felt was shameful.

Elise.

"Okay."

"I'm serious, Sloane. If you need a break, speak up."

I hadn't been nervous about talking to Wilson and Cole but now I was.

"I said okay, Asher."

He looked like he had more to say—no, he looked like he was holding his body tight like he was fighting the urge to touch me. Or maybe that was wishful thinking—my silly, love-struck heart wanting him to reach over and pull me into his arms.

"Okay," he whispered.

With more force than necessary, I opened my door and all but flung myself out of the car. I followed Asher to the front door, grateful he couldn't see my scowl—or more apt, my pout.

This time when I walked in, there was no greeting. Wilson was at the huge dining table with a laptop open, papers stacked around him, and while I couldn't see him in his entirety he didn't appear to be in a suit.

"Where's Cole?" Asher inquired.

Wilson jerked his head toward the open door to the back deck. "Run. He should be back any minute."

The vibe in the room was anything but friendly, which of course made Asher's warning more ominous.

"Want something to drink? Coffee? Water?"

A shot of tequila, I thought.

"Water, please."

"Wilson?"

Without taking his eyes off me Wilson answered, "I'm good."

Asher broke off to get my water, leaving me standing alone under Wilson's watchful stare. I was not getting a good feeling about this.

"Have a seat." Wilson dipped his chin indicating the chair across from him.

I walked woodenly to the table and pulled out the chair. Before my butt made it to the seat Asher was back setting a bottle of water on the table in front of me. I didn't want to acknowledge how much his presence calmed me, but it did, especially when Wilson was studying me like I was the last person on the planet he wanted to see.

"Any word on Lorenzo?" Asher launched in.

I didn't miss the tiny jump in Wilson's cheek at the mention of my boss's son.

"Yes, his secretary got back to me. I'm meeting with him tomorrow."

"And the party?" Asher continued. "Does Sloane still need to put something together?"

The party? I figured that was bullshit, part of Adam's plan to get me to go out to dinner with him.

Wilson's gaze sliced to Asher, and I was happy for the reprieve. Wilson was intense, his eyes cold, posture menacing. The man obviously didn't like me though I had no clue why.

"No need."

There was some form of silent man-communication between Asher and Wilson. If the vibe was chilly before, it was downright frosty now—suffocatingly so. I was still in the process of plucking up the nerve to question what was going on when I caught sight of Cole on the deck—shirtless and sweaty from his run.

Sweet mother of pearl. There was no denying Cole was good-looking with his messy mop of dark brown hair and blue eyes, but the sweat rolling down his chest upped the hotness factor a few notches. I'd always preferred my men clean-shaven or with a little bit of stubble like Asher wore but for the first time in my life, I was contemplating the sex appeal of a full, bushy beard. However, my consideration was cut short when the fog lifted, and I realized Cole's lips were downturned into a fierce scowl.

Oh no, not him, too.

But as soon as Cole turned his head and his gaze collided with mine his features transformed—lightning quick the foreboding frown and creases between his eyebrows disappeared. In their place was a carefree expression as he leisurely strolled into the house.

"Damn, brother," Cole snickered. "You said she clocked you, not that she bested you." Cole's lips twitched and he tossed me a flirty wink as he made his way into the kitchen.

"It was one lucky punch," Asher grumbled.

Wilson's gaze remained cool and alert as one brow arched. He didn't look pleased that I took a shot at Asher—as a matter of fact, he looked downright pissed he was being forced to breathe the same air as me.

What the hell?

Who did he think he was? Wilson had no reason to be mad at me. I'd done nothing wrong and if he was mad that I punched his coworker and couldn't understand at the time I was in fear for my life then he could fuck right off.

"It wasn't a lucky shot," I started. "But he is lucky I punched him before he taught me how to bust a nut or there's a strong possibility he'd never have kids." A thought struck me, and I turned from Wilson to Asher to ask, "Wait, do you have kids?"

Asher's lips were pinched together tightly, the sides of his eyes crinkled, and he was shaking his head.

"No, sweetness, I don't have any kids."

I didn't know why that was such a relief but it was. Not that I didn't like kids, I did. I actually hoped in the future I'd have a few but the thought of Asher loving someone enough to reproduce with them made my stomach knot. Stupid, I know, but I felt it all the same.

Then suddenly the air in the room changed. It filled with a deep, rumbling laugh followed by a loud bang on the table. I jumped at the sound and my gaze sliced to Wilson. His head was tipped to the side, his lips were parted but upturned and he was laughing. No, he was hysterically laughing while slapping his hand on the table.

"Bust a nut?" Cole asked around a chuckle. "Do tell how Asher taught you how to bust a nut."

"Grab, squeeze, and twist."

"Grab, squeeze, and twist," Cole repeated. "That'll do it."

"I'm not fond of the twisting part until they pop," I informed Cole. "But I'm less fond of being—"

"Baby," Asher cut me off.

"Holy shit," Cole sputtered. "But the popping part's the best."

What?

"Cole," Asher warned.

"Brother, she opened the door. Not only that she walked right through it," Cole returned.

I what?

"What's he talking about?"

For some reason my question made all three men burst out laughing. It took longer than it should've for realization to dawn, but when it did I felt my cheeks heat until they were ready to catch fire.

Bust a nut.

Did I seriously say that?

"I didn't..." I started but faltered. "That's not..." Another start and stop. "Not *that* kind of nut-busting."

Cole howled. Wilson chuckled. Asher smiled.

"Seriously?" I snapped. "How old are you?"

"A man is never too old to laugh at a good nut joke," Cole informed me.

"He's not wrong." Wilson smiled.

"Well, if you don't stop laughing at me you might find yourself busting a nut."

"That will never fucking happen," Asher growled.

My gaze slowly moved through Wilson and Cole until it landed on Asher.

"How do you know I wasn't talking to you? You're laughing at me right along with them."

"Good Lord," Cole boomed. "I might not bust a nut but I'm gonna bust a gut."

"No one's busting a nut," Asher announced.

That was when I lost it and joined in the laughter.

Wilson smiled at me and my nerves started to settle.

More sadness crept over me unexpectedly. Elise would love these guys' sense of humor. Out of the two of us, she was the funny one. She was the one with the quick come-back. I was the sidekick, the wingwoman, the one along for the ride. Back before Elise went missing I might've been wild and crazy but she was wild*er*, craz*ier*, she was up for anything while I had my limits.

Asher's laughter faded as did his smile. I felt his hand hit my thigh, his fingers softly curled in, then he gave me a gentle squeeze. Which left me wondering what I had done in my life that was so horrible the universe would put Asher in my path only to take him away. What had I done to deserve to have all that was him dangled in front of me during the shittiest time in my life?

He had all the makings of perfection, but I'd never know the reality of him.

My ringing phone cut off my musing and plunged the rest of the room into silence, evaporating the happy vibe.

"I should get that."

I leaned to the side to grab my phone out of my back pocket which brought me closer to Asher. His head was turned to the side, his eyes tipped down. Mine tipped up, and when our eyes collided I found it hard to breathe. It wasn't his good looks that stole my breath, it wasn't the remnants of his cologne, it wasn't his lips being close to mine. It was his understanding gaze. It was the mutual desire, the knowledge that we both felt the same puzzling pull of the other. But it was also the melancholy.

Bad timing.

Once I had my phone out, I lost Asher's eyes as we both looked down at the screen.

Lorenzo.

"Speaker, sweetness, I wanna hear what he has to say."

It might've been the 'sweetness' or the fact I could give

two shits who heard the call but without argument, I accepted the call and placed it on speaker.

"Hello?"

"Sloane."

In some sort of fucked up cosmic joke, the universe had seen fit to give Lorenzo Kelly, otherwise known as Disgusting Pig a smooth, deep, sexy voice. For months he'd creeped me out. Now I knew why—he wasn't disgusting, he was totally depraved.

"Yes, Lorenzo. How may I help you?"

"I need you to come in early."

Shit. I was afraid that was what he was going to say.

"Is there a problem?"

"No. I've invited some VIPs for tonight's party and I want to go over specifics. You also need to arrange for Sammy to come in tonight. They'll need a private hostess for the evening."

Sammy was a bright-eyed blonde who worked at Club Joi as a way to take care of her ailing father. She was also young and took advantage of the club's amenities which meant he wanted her specifically because he was a sick fuck.

"I'll see what I can do but Sammy's been on vacation for a week. Maybe Marla can come in."

"No Marla. She's too fat. Tell Sammy there's a thousand-dollar bonus in it for her."

Prick! Marla's not fat.

I felt the bile inch up my throat but before I could think of another girl who was not on shift I could suggest, Asher lightly tapped the table, drawing my attention to him.

He silently shook his head. I returned with a swift shake of mine, to which he replied with another shake.

He wanted me to stop arguing and call in Sammy.

I wanted to call in anyone other than the sweet, young girl who was willing to do anything to help her father with medical bills, which included taking tips from couples when she acted as a third. Something that was dangerously close to prostitution.

"Sloane?" Lorenzo's impatient voice hit my ears and I wanted to vomit.

"I can be there in an hour, we'll discuss it then."

Asher's eyes narrowed, his brows furrowed, and his lips thinned.

What the hell?

I tilted my head in question, his eyes narrowed further, and confusion set in.

"Good. Everything needs to be perfect for tonight."

"It will be," I assured him, barely holding back the retching sound threatening to accompany my promise.

Lorenzo disconnected the call and Asher seethed. "You'll be there in an hour?"

"Well, yeah. That's how long it normally takes me to get to work from The Valley. I didn't think you wanted him to know I was hanging out with you down the road."

Asher grunted something unintelligible, then clear as day he made his demand.

"You're quitting."

"Quitting what?"

"The club," he growled.

I was not quitting the club. After nearly seven months of working in a sex club, Lorenzo had finally shown his true colors. I was getting closer to finding out what happened to Elise and my money was on the slimeball.

"I'm not quitting the club."

"You are."

My mouth opened and closed at least a dozen times before I found the proper words.

"No, I'm fucking not."

"You are, Sloane. You heard Lorenzo last night. He's arranging for me to *buy* a girl. He's dangerous."

I didn't miss the way Asher spat out the word *buy*. I also didn't miss the hatred in his voice.

"I'm not stupid, Asher. I know he's dangerous."

I watched as Asher's frame grew stiff, his face contorted, and I braced for his fury. But it never came. Something else passed over him. Defeat? I couldn't exactly place the emotion before it was gone.

His face was carefully blank when he asked, "Has he ever asked you to plan a VIP party before?"

What? That was it? After he'd demanded I quit, he was giving up? That easy.

I should've been elated that Asher was moving the conversation on—there was no way in hell I was going to quit. But instead, I was strangely disappointed.

"No," I answered. "The closest I've come is setting up a private viewing for a Platinum member."

"What's a private viewing?" Cole asked.

"The member wanted an erotic show," I explained.

"Still not tracking what a show is."

It was too early in the day to be discussing the ins and outs of an erotic sex show. No, strike that, there was never a time during the day or night when I wanted to discuss my job duties at the club. Sometimes my job was blessedly normal—ordering food and liquor, scheduling the staff, and checking the rooms were cleaned and stocked. Those were the times I could pretend I worked for a hotel or some rich guy who liked to throw parties five nights a week. Of course, that normalcy dissolved when the members arrived and clothes came off. But for the most part, I could lie to myself that I hadn't sunk into a world where I didn't belong.

"The member wanted three women, all blondes, to dance for him. His rules were they didn't touch him. He got to direct the action. The setup of that was easy; all I had to do was clear a room and schedule the women."

To my surprise Cole's nose scrunched up, making him look adorably disturbed.

"Where did you find the women?" Wilson joined the conversation.

One would think after all the months I'd worked around nudity and sex I would've become ambivalent about the whole scene. Yet, I still found it difficult to talk about my job.

"Like Sammy, the girls I called in work at the club. There are no outsiders allowed in except during the yearly masquerade ball. I, however, haven't worked at the club long enough to attend one, I just know that extra staff is hired for the evening."

"Why are you averse to calling in Sammy?" Wilson continued to question me.

"She's young."

"The tall blonde? Sammy Price?" Asher asked.

Of course, he knew who I was talking about. Not only was Sammy beautiful but he'd also taken notice of her age.

"Yes. She's barely twenty and only there to help pay for her father's medical bills. I can't deny she enjoys herself when she's there and off shift, but I can't help wondering if she's using the club and sex to escape from her problems. The other women who work there are different."

As soon as I finished my statement, I realized how bad that sounded and quickly rushed to explain, "The others are older, more world-wise. They sought employment at the club for the free membership. It's clear they're into the scene and were before they started working there. Sammy's there because it pays well, and she can spend all day helping her father."

Wilson's eyes transferred to Asher. Mine followed and when they landed on Asher his jaw was clenched.

"What's wrong?" I asked.

"Nothing," Asher lied. "You've got forty minutes before you have to leave for work. Before you do, let's go over Elise."

My heart rate immediately accelerated. This was it, Asher was going to help.

"What do you want to know?"

"Everything. Start from the beginning."

The beginning.

I could do that.

Cole sat himself at the table, bare chest and all. Wilson pulled out a pad of paper and nabbed a pen. Asher relaxed his jaw and settled in. Then I started at the beginning and told the guys everything I knew about my best friend.

15

"CALM THE HELL DOWN," Wilson clipped.

Calm? Fuck calm. Sloane had been picked up by an Uber and left to go to the club over six hours ago. Six fucking hours of her being alone with Lorenzo—calm was not an option. My head was so full of the multitude of vile, disgusting things that motherfucker could've been doing to her, I had no room left to think about anything else—not Elise, not the effort I'd made to look deeper into her friend's disappearance, not the side-eye I'd caught Sloane giving a shirtless Cole, not the jealousy that spiked, not my reaction to Sloane's stubborn denial.

I thought Sloane would've been relieved she could quit the club. Hell, I was relieved at the thought of her quitting the club and cutting ties with Lorenzo. I needed her far away from the motherfucker so I could keep my eye on the prize—taking him down. Not keeping one eye on her and the other on the scumbag who offered to sell me some poor woman's virginity.

Fuck!

I could get her fired.

I continued to drum my fingers on the table as I contemplated the option. It would be easy—a total dick move, but easy. Club Joi valued their members over their employees. A simple complaint about Sloane and she'd be free from danger. She'd also be pissed as fuck.

"Whatever it is you're over there thinking about," Cole began, "it's a bad idea."

I turned to look at my friend and asked, "Why would you say that?"

"Because you stopped the tapping and now you look constipated."

I flipped him an obscene gesture before I announced, "I'm gonna get her fired."

"*Who* are you gonna get fired?" Cole slowly drawled.

"Uh... Sloane."

"Yeah, that's who I was afraid you were talking about."

"It's the perfect—"

"Way to get your ass kicked," Wilson finished my sentence.

"Lorenzo is—"

I was again cut off by Wilson. "Going to be taken down."

"You don't—"

"Understand?"

My annoyance sparked and I snapped.

"Stop fucking cutting me off."

"Then stop thinking crazy, calm the fuck down, and go get ready to go to work."

The cool ocean breeze coming in from the open French doors did nothing to calm me. Nothing to settle the riot of nerves bundled in my chest. Nothing to soothe the worry.

After months of working at the club, we finally had a lead. But it was just a start and there was no telling how deep it went. Was Lorenzo acting on his own, selling girls on the side, or was his father involved? Were there other members who went to Lorenzo to sate their perversions? And there was Elise and the girl who reportedly ran the grounds naked. The woman none of the staff had seen.

I pushed back from the table and stood looking at Wilson. "We need to dig deeper into the staff members who were questioned by the police?"

"We did. They came up clean," Wilson reminded me.

"Then we missed something. After the club closes a cleaning crew comes in," I told him something he knew. Not only was the club's schedule in my reports but Wilson and Cole had both watched the mansion overnight. "Every morning one of the groundskeepers works outside, there's a day maid, and the chef comes in early afternoon. If a woman was held at the mansion after the club closed there's no way someone didn't see her there, especially if she was running around outside naked. Even if the gardener missed her, that house has three-hundred-sixty-five views of the property—the day maid would have. And where did she go? Who went out to get her? Where was she kept? Someone working that day saw her. Someone had to have heard her. And she didn't just vanish, someone took her off that property. I don't believe Lorenzo is working this by himself. He's got someone inside that club."

"Could be a member," Cole tossed out.

"Could be. But my gut's telling me it's staff. That's not to say there aren't members who are buying what he's selling on the side."

My stomach clenched at the thought of Sloane being in the mix of men who were possibly at the club for more than a good time. Men with dark souls who would sink to the shadiest pits of depravity. Getting her fired was sounding better and better. Wilson was right—she'd be pissed as all fuck, taking away her control. Her ability to act out her steadfast loyalty to her friend would lead Sloane to never speak to me again.

But she'd be safe.

And in a few weeks, I'd be gone and she'd go back to her life and we'd forever be separated by distance. So what did I care if that separation came early? She'd be out of Lorenzo's sight. She'd be clear of the danger.

"You've gone back there," Cole rightly surmised. "I don't get it. For months you've done nothing but try to convince us that Sloane's clean. Now you wanna put her out of commission when we can use her? She has access to things you don't."

"We're not using Sloane for anything. I want her out of there."

"You're thinking with your dick, brother."

How wrong Cole was. I was thinking with my heart. I was thinking that if Sloane got hurt or worse, turned up like her friend, I would lose my fucking mind and burn that mansion to the ground. I'd maim and kill and not think twice.

Unable to explain what I was feeling without giving away I'd fallen for a woman who I barely knew, I did the only thing I could do. I flipped my teammate the middle finger and started toward my bedroom. But I stopped in the hallway and turned back.

"Do me a favor. The next time Sloane's over, put on a fucking shirt."

My demand said it all, gave away what I was trying to hide, yet I couldn't find it in me to care.

"Jealous?" Cole smirked.

"Red with it," I admitted.

"Not green?" Cole quipped.

"Green would imply I'm envious," I corrected.

After the initial shock of seeing Cole come back shirt-less from his run, Sloane had settled in and ignored Cole's state of undress. She hadn't stared at his chest or given him lingering looks. She'd seemed more concerned about Wilson's grumpy disposition. The man in the suit had her on edge. Yet I couldn't stop the jealousy and possessiveness from gnawing at my insides. It was all I could do to keep myself in check when I watched her work. I knew what she saw. Every night. Every room she entered. Sex in all forms that sex could be had. I didn't need my brother, my team-mate, my friend adding to my growing frustration.

———

I PARKED my car and scanned the lot. It was earlier than when I normally showed up yet there were already twice as many cars.

Fuck.

I shot off a text to Wilson informing him of the situation and added as many license plates as I could see from the safety of my BMW. When I got back his reply, I deleted the text and shoved the phone under the front seat and grabbed my work phone. If shit went down and my car was searched all they'd find was a burner phone with no calls, no texts. If someone looked through my work phone, they'd find plenty. Fake calls and texts to fake colleagues courtesy of Shep. I shoved the phone into the inside pocket of my suit jacket and exited the car.

There would be a great many benefits to this assign-ment being over. The top of the list would be taking down another scumbag. The side effect to that but equally important would be to save innocent women from horrible fates. Another plus would be getting Sloane the answers she wanted—however, I feared they were not going to be the ones we wanted. And if by some miracle after close to seven months of being held against her will, used the way I knew sex trafficked victims were used, if Elise was still alive, she would not now or ever be the same woman Sloane knew.

Way down on the list of bonuses would be shedding the suits. I didn't like wearing them when I was in the FBI and I liked them even less now after years of not having to wear them with Takeback. Wilson was the frontman. He was the one who sat in on meetings with government officials. Even outside of work, it was a rare occasion to see him slumming it in jeans and a tee.

By the time I made it to the front door of the mansion the hair on the back of my neck was standing on end. After I checked in and handed over my phone to Dee, tonight's greeter, a ball of unease had solidly knotted in my gut. Men I'd never seen before lingered in the massive living room. Ten of them were sharply dressed, all with tumblers of amber liquid. Three men I didn't recognize were off to the side, hanging back with no drinks. Private security for the VIPs.

"Adam," Lorenzo greeted before I could get a lock on Sloane.

I took a breath, exhaled my annoyance, and returned, "Lorenzo. Nice to see you."

"I was hoping you'd be here tonight."

"Oh? Why's that?"

"Are you still interested? You know, in *sweetness*?"

Fucking pig.

"Yes, I remember, seeing as we had that conversation

last night." I paused to lean in close. "Though I'm unclear why you'd discuss such a matter here."

"You have nothing to fear if—"

Stupid fucking asshole.

"If this is how you conduct business, I'm no longer interested."

I backed away with the intention of finding Sloane but halted at Lorenzo's words.

"She's not here," he sneered.

His words slammed into my chest before they bounced around in my head, making my vision momentarily haze.

"Come again?"

"Miss Ellis," he confirmed my fear. "She's not here."

The need for answers barely offset my desire to wrap my hands around the asshole's throat until I choked the life out of him.

My gaze went over Lorenzo's shoulder to the three men standing guard, alert but relaxed. I kept a cool mask of indifference firmly in place and glanced back at Lorenzo.

"I'm unclear why you'd feel the need to inform me of Miss Ellis's whereabouts."

A nasty smile from Lorenzo sent chills up my spine.

"I've seen you watching her. I don't blame you, she's a very beautiful woman. Though I'm surprised."

My blood was reaching boiling. This conversation needed to end before I said or did something that would blow my cover. Unfortunately, Lorenzo had more to say.

"She's a prude." He chuckled. "Or she's a cock tease. I haven't figured her out yet. I should've fired her months ago but she's good at her job." His nasty smile turned into a leer, and I braced. "I suppose I understand a man taking what he can get while he waits for what he needs."

Yep. My blood was boiling.

"I don't need to *take* what's freely given," I returned, modulating my voice.

"So you've fucked her?"

The boiling in my veins was nearing critical mass. I was backed into a corner, which was a dangerous place for a man like me. I was leashed due to the investigation. One misstep and I'd blow the whole operation.

Thankfully I was saved by a tall, leggy, barely dressed woman who'd caught Lorenzo's attention.

"I'll meet you in my office in thirty minutes," Lorenzo told me as he stepped away. "Oh, and Miss Ellis is downstairs finishing up the VIP lounge. Feel free to help yourself."

She's not here.

Fucking pig.

The relief I felt that Sloane was in the mansion did nothing to quell the burn in my gut. Lorenzo was careless but he wasn't stupid. He'd caught on to my interest in Sloane.

I'd been played.

Fuck.

Not wanting to give away more than I had, I waited for Lorenzo to follow the woman into one of the viewing rooms before I made my way to the stairs. In my desperation to find Sloane, I disregarded operational protocol. What I should've done and what I did were vastly different. I hit the bottom of the stairs and scanned the room knowing I should've stayed upstairs with my eyes on Lorenzo's guests. I should've been getting close, watching, listening, learning. Instead my need to lay eyes on Sloane and confirm her whereabouts only reinforced my decision. I needed her gone. She was the distraction I couldn't afford. And if I couldn't talk some sense into her, I'd get her away from

Club Joi by any means necessary. I'd welcome her anger for the peace of mind knowing she was free and clear of danger would bring me. I'd ignore her sadness and my broken heart and settle knowing that she would live a long, safe life hating me.

Fuck.

16

THIS WAS NOT RIGHT.

Actually, there was so much wrong with this that I couldn't find a single thing to latch onto to make myself feel better about what I was doing.

Lorenzo hadn't waited for me to come to the mansion to discuss the VIP party and which girl would be the hostess. When I'd arrived, Sammy was already in Lorenzo's office along with a woman who I'd never met. After a quick introduction to Adria, Lorenzo informed me she was a professional Dominatrix and would be tonight's VIP entertainment.

Ten minutes later, Lorenzo walked us downstairs through the common area known as the hunting ground, down the short janitorial hallway, and stopped. Sammy looked unsure but when Lorenzo opened a hidden door the poor girl started shifting from side to side. When we stepped inside and the lights came on my stomach dropped and Sammy turned sheet white. Lorenzo didn't notice seeing as he was too busy ushering Adria around the room.

The room?

More like a torture chamber.

Not like the room in those sexy movies. Oh no, not like that at all. It wasn't red. It didn't have a big four-poster bed. No troubled hot guy ready to fuck you into oblivion. Nope. Not like that at all. The only thing the rooms had in common was that pain would be inflicted.

One side of the room had slats running horizontally from wall to wall with spaces between the long pieces of wood. There were metal eye hooks screwed into the wood in random places. Or maybe not so randomly. Maybe they were perfectly placed to chain or tie or cuff a woman to the wall. An abundance of chains, ropes, and cuffs hung on the wall to the right of the wall of pain. To the left whips, paddles, crops, and other leather instruments I couldn't begin to name. Ten black leather chairs were arranged in the middle of the room facing the slatted wall.

I could barely breathe as I took it all in.

Sammy stood silently next to me, and I knew the minute she'd accepted her fate. Her shoulders hunched forward, her eyes cast downward to the hardwood floor, and she blew out a long, slow breath.

I said nothing while Lorenzo explained the evening he'd planned.

Which begged the question of why the hell he called me into work early to plan a party when he'd already had everything worked out.

Then there was Adria. Not even two hours ago I told Asher, Wilson, and Cole the club didn't hire outsiders. The woman certainly didn't work at the club, and I'd never seen her attend a Soiree, though she could be an inactive member.

I had been confused, pissed, and I hated to admit it even to myself, scared.

After Lorenzo and Adria worked out a few kinks —*pardon the pun*—we were dismissed. As soon as Lorenzo had left Sammy and me upstairs in the huge living room I tried to broach the evening with Sammy. She'd immediately shot me down and told me she needed the money.

Out of fear that Sammy had no idea what she was getting herself into even though Lorenzo had explained in great detail how Sammy would be the one secured to the wall while Adria the Dominatrix worked her over—whatever the hell that meant—I offered to give Sammy the thousand dollars if she called out. She met my offer with a sweet smile and denial.

Sweet Sammy was going to do it.

She was going to allow a woman she did not know chain her to a wall and beat her for the entertainment of a group of men who'd get off on hearing her cry and beg.

This next part was a mistake.

I called an Uber and went home to change for work. I didn't do what I should've done and called Asher to tell him what was going on. I should've called to tell him there was a secret room I knew nothing about, which meant there could be more rooms.

Torture chambers.

I didn't call because I was being stubborn. I knew telling him would only give him more ammunition and another demand I quit. Which, hindsight being what it was, I should've listened to Asher and quit over the phone. I should never have gone to the club early. I never should've met Adria. I never should've seen the wall of pain.

I also didn't call on my drive back to the club.

Now was now, and I was helping Sammy get the room ready for the VIPs. You know, the normal—towels in the warmer, lube, condoms, nipple clamps.

"These tumblers have spots," Sammy said, holding a glass up to the light.

God forbid a tumbler had a water spot when there was probably leftover ejaculate somewhere in the room from a previous party.

"Listen, Sammy—"

"I'm fine."

She was not fine. She'd been quiet and tense since we'd started setting up the room.

"Let me take your place."

No sooner did the words come out of my mouth than Sammy's laughter bounced around the room. I would swear the sound rattled the torture apparatuses hanging on the walls. She was no closer to settling down when I continued.

"Seriously, let me take your place?"

"Girl," she sang.

Now I was getting offended. She either thought I was too weak to handle a solid paddling, or she thought I was a buttoned-up puritan.

"What?"

Sammy sobered and gave me a half grin. "I appreciate your offer. I really appreciate why you're offering. It's sweet. But, I'm fine. I admit I was shocked at first." Sammy paused and her cheeks shaded pink. "I've done some of this. Never with a woman, but I've done it. After we're done here I'm meeting with Mistress Adria to go over safe words and protocol."

Safe words and protocol.

Jesus.

"Promise?"

"Promise," Sammy parroted.

With nothing else to say, I sighed and gave up.

"Go and get ready. I'll finish here and restock the glasses."

"You sure?" she asked.

I glanced at the complicated shiny, pleather outfit Sammy still needed to change into crumpled on a chair and nodded.

"Yeah, girl. You're gonna need a minute to strap into that thing."

Plus, she had safe words to go over, and I was thinking those were pretty important.

"Thanks, Sloane. You're the best."

With that, she snatched up the outfit and rushed out.

I did not. I walked over to the built-in cabinet and took my time opening and closing all the drawers. All of them were empty. I ran my hand along the slatted wall, pushing and pulling, and did the same on the toy wall. I wasn't sure what I was looking for—another hidden room, a lever that made the built-in swing open to a secret vault, anything.

Unsurprisingly I came up empty. I'd also wasted time playing amateur sleuth. In less than an hour, the VIPs would be coming down for their show. I grabbed the box of dirty tumblers and made my way out of the room but stopped midway down the hall when I heard voices.

"Tonight," voice number one demanded.

"Patience," the other man spat harshly.

I was getting ready to resume my steps when man number two spoke again and sent my world spiraling. "Do not push me on this. You fucked up with the other one. I told you, only the ones with no family. No one to miss them."

Oh my God. Were they talking about Elise? No one to miss them? I missed her, and so did her parents.

"Doesn't matter who misses her, they're never gonna find her."

I strained to listen over the buzzing in my ears. I prayed my legs wouldn't give out and give away my presence. My hands were shaking so badly I feared the tumblers inside would start rattling and they'd find me.

"Do not touch her," voice number two ordered. "She lives with her father. He'll report her missing by morning. Lorenzo has someone set up."

Sammy.

They're talking about sweet Sammy.

Holy shit.

I had to find Asher—no, Mr. Newcomb. He was Adam Newcomb in the club. I couldn't screw that up.

Adam Newcomb I repeated in my head as I stepped back, thankful for the carpet in the hallway. Another silent step back. And another. By the time I made it back into the dungeon I was out of breath, panting, and my entire body was trembling. Fear and adrenaline clashed and churned in my stomach, each emotion warring for the top spot, making me feel woozy.

I needed Asher, but first I needed to find a way out undetected. Or a distraction, something to alert the men I was in the room so they'd stop their conversation and move on.

Before I could decide on a plan of action the box slipped from my hands. In those seconds as I watched the box fall to the floor, I stood there like an idiot. I didn't come up with a plan. I didn't run. I didn't find a place to hide. Nope, not me. I froze. I didn't even startle when the glasses inside the box shattered.

I didn't move when I heard footsteps coming down the

hall, but I did lift my gaze when voice number two softly asked, "Are you okay?"

Will Evans.

My mind spun as I tried to recall everything I knew about the man. Longtime member, unattached, liked to join in when invited into a threesome, spent time in the viewing rooms but I'd never seen him pleasured.

God, how was this my life—self-pleasure, walls of pain, threesomes. Then there was overhearing nefarious plots to kidnap my coworker.

I totally should've listened to Asher—that was strike one. I should've called him when I had a bad feeling about Lorenzo calling me in early for no reason—that was strike two.

"Miss Ellis?"

Hurry, idiot, think up a lie.

"Yes, I'm sorry. I forgot to eat today, and I started to feel lightheaded. I guess I dropped the box."

Mr. Evans looked around the room before his concerned eyes came back to mine.

"Are you sure that's it?"

Think, lie again. More lies, think.

"Please don't tell Mr. Kelly."

Mr. Evans kept his eyes locked with mine and took a step closer, making my heart rate speed up.

"What would I tell Mr. Kelly?"

"That I interrupted your night. Again, I'm so sorry to have bothered you. I don't know exactly what happened. One second, I was going over my mental to-do list making sure I hadn't forgotten anything important. Everything has to be perfect. Then the next thing I knew I was swaying on my feet and dropped the box." I stopped to let out an overexaggerated sigh in hopes of making my story more believable. "Now I need to get the cleaner down here to make sure no glass escaped from the box. Someone could get injured. Someone could—"

"Take a breath, sweetheart."

Gross.

I did as he suggested and gave him a fake lopsided smile that probably looked more like I was constipated, but at that point as long as he didn't kill me or strap me to the wall, I didn't care what my face looked like. Luckily, Will seemed to buy my wobbly grin.

"I can't tell you how—"

"Stop, Sloane," he interrupted my apology. "There's no need to be sorry. I was on my way to the restroom when I heard the commotion."

"Oh, well, the restrooms are on the other side of the bar," I helpfully chirped. "I can show you the way if you'd like."

"I'm well aware of the location." He chuckled.

"Right, of course."

Will clucked his tongue and dipped his chin toward the box. "Where does this need to go?"

"The trash."

"Yes, I assumed so. Is there one door here big enough for the box or would you like me to carry it upstairs for you?"

"Oh, I couldn't ask—"

"You didn't. I offered."

Before I could ask, movement at the door caught my attention. My eyes moved over Will's shoulder and relief swept through me right before panic set in.

Asher—no, Adam.

Shit. I was going to mess this up.

Will turned to see what I was staring at and once again I was frozen as the temperature in the room rose significantly.

Asher's eyes flitted to mine for a moment before settling back on Will.

Shit. Fuck. And damn.

What was I supposed to do now?

Your job! Play it cool.

"Mr. Newcomb, may I help you with something?"

There. I used the correct name.

"I've been looking for you," Asher replied.

His steel-like tone took me by surprise and since I didn't know what to make of it or what to say to his declaration, I wasn't sure how I was supposed to proceed.

"I'm being rude," I announced. "Mr. Evans, do you know Mr. Newcomb?"

"Yes, we've met."

Neither man moved to shake the other's hand, which I suppose in a place like this wasn't unheard of. You never knew where that hand had been or what was on it.

Yep, this was my life. Public masturbation and sticky hands.

Awesome. Perfect. I should've quit this afternoon.

What the hell happened now?

Should I say something? Move? Stay silent in the hopes that Will left?

"If you're done here, play has started and I believe we had scheduled time," Asher weirdly said.

Scheduled time?

The wheels in my head began to rotate until everything clicked.

This was my out.

"I didn't realize I was holding you up," Will smoothly interjected. "Now it is I who must apologize to you for interrupting your playtime." He bent and picked up the box of broken glass. "I'll take this and discard it. And don't worry, *sweetheart*, my lips are sealed."

A shiver of disgust crawled up my throat when Will brushed his hand over my shoulder before he sauntered across the room. My gaze shifted to Asher—his was aimed at the spot Will had touched. Jaw clenched, eyes narrowed, bolts of hostility might as well have been sparking off him he was so pissed.

I opened my mouth but before I got any words out Asher lunged and hooked me around the waist. One second, he was standing across the room the next he had me pressed against him with his mouth close to my ear.

"No talking," he whispered. "You get me?" I nodded once and he continued. "We're going up. And it seriously fucks me to say this, but we're going in a viewing room."

Tension coiled so tight in my stomach that I'd no longer be lying if I said I was dizzy.

"Sweetness, you know," Asher growled softly. "You fucking know that shit does nothing for me. This isn't about that. It's about me covering you until you can get out of here. And you doing the same for me."

He was right—I knew he didn't get off on watching and neither did I, but down in the darkest recesses of my mind I wondered if that was because I'd never watched with *him*.

"I know," I whispered back.

"When I walked in you looked scared." He was still speaking in low tones, and I was beginning to wonder if he was worried there were cameras in the room.

I wouldn't put it past Lorenzo.

In lieu of answering, I nodded again.

"Did he threaten you?"

I shook my head.

"But he scared you?"

"I heard something." Asher's body went solid against mine.

"Not here."

Oh, yeah, he totally thought there were cameras in here.

As soon as I acknowledged his directive his face came away from my ear and as it did his lips brushed over the hinge of my jaw, over my cheek, and in a barely there sweep they grazed over my lips. That might've been the single sexiest sorta-kiss I'd ever experienced. And since I'd kissed Asher—really kissed him—I knew how he could steal my breath with a single swipe of his tongue, so that was saying something. I'd also had the pleasure of him bringing me to orgasm and still that lip sweep was more intimate.

"You look beautiful tonight," he said in a normal tone of voice. I lamely stared up at him not yet recovered when Asher broke the spell. "Before we go up do you remember what I told you?"

He told me a lot of things in the last twenty-four hours, none of which I could remember with him so close.

I blinked. Asher didn't, his eyes stayed glued to mine while he finished shattering the illusion. "You may watch but no touching. I do not share. Period."

The cameras.

Everything in my life was a lie.

The lip brush was fake.

I desperately wished that it was real.

———

THIS HAD to be rock bottom. Only it wasn't jagged, sharp edges of stone I felt. It was Asher's chest against my back. It was his strong thighs under my ass. It was his hand on my hip and his chin on my shoulder as he watched the couple on the platform in front of us.

As soon as we entered the viewing room, he led us to a chair off to the side and insisted I sit on his lap. I wasn't sure if it was for show or if being in his lap with his arm clasping me to him was a way of protecting me. Either way, it was hell.

The woman in front of us arched her back and moaned. It wasn't the sound of her satisfaction that had me wiggling, it wasn't the man's mouth between her legs, it wasn't her naked breasts or his bare ass. It was jealousy. I didn't want to perform in front of a group of people, I never wanted to be on display, but I wanted to feel what she was feeling. Just once I wanted to know what it felt like to be worshiped, pleasured beyond rational thought. I wanted Asher between my legs. I wanted to get lost in his touch. I wanted to make him lose himself. I wanted to fall asleep next to him sweaty and exhausted and wake up next to him energized so we could start again.

But that was never going to happen. He would leave and I'd be stuck in a life that was mediocre at best. I'd have average sex, I'd find an average job, I'd have to find new friends since I'd lost all of mine and they'd be average, too. My one chance at extraordinary would be in Idaho living his best life and, in a few weeks, I'd be nothing more than a passing memory.

This had to be the absolute lowest. There could be no further to fall, there couldn't possibly be another level in which I could sink. Asher proved my thoughts wrong when he slid his hand from my hip to my stomach and then up between my breasts, stopping only when it was around my throat just under my jaw. His mouth went to my neck and his tongue traced a line up to my ear, causing me to tremble.

The pressure on my throat intensified as Asher used his grip to tilt my head back.

"I'm trying so fucking hard, sweetness." He punched out each word, the blow of them knocking the wind out of me. "Stop. Moving."

Then with his breath fanning over my neck, I sank deeper into the hell I created. The nightmare that was my life. The dream that would never come to pass. The fantasy that was Asher.

"Any other place, any other time, your dress would be around your hips, my cock would be buried so... *fucking...* deep and you'd be screaming for more."

Try as I might to remind myself this was all an act—providing Asher cover while he worked—I failed. A whimper slipped past my lips and I felt no regret, no shame, no need to call it back and pretend I was unaffected.

"You had your chance," I reminded him.

"No, sweetness, I had the chance to fuck you." He paused and scraped his teeth down the sensitive skin under my ear. "I want to *own* you. I want you to need me like you need your next breath. I want you delirious. I want you begging. And if I can't have that, if I can't keep you, if I can't give you everything I have, then I want nothing."

Later I'd condemn my wildly inappropriate musings. Later I'd worry about the repercussions. Later I'd stitch my heart back together after I gave myself a moment to imagine what it would be like to have Asher give me everything.

The room melted away. The cries of the woman in front of me, the grunts of exhortation from the man licking her into a frenzy faded to nothingness and I drifted to the other time, the place where Asher and I were alone—my dress around my hips, his cock buried deep, me screaming his name, begging for more. Unconsciously I clenched my thighs seeking relief from the ache he'd caused. In my altered state of mind, I could feel his lips on mine, his tongue exploring, his hands roaming in his quest to own my body.

"You make yourself come, baby, and all bets are off," he rasped.

I wanted all bets to be off. I wanted him to carry me into one of the privacy rooms and make good on the empty promises he'd threatened.

"If you don't want me to come by myself then you better—"

"Sloane."

My name sounded like an invocation, a beautiful, torturous plea to show mercy. However, I was too far gone, too deep in the illusion of our moment.

"I'm close," I whispered.

From one breath to the next Asher was on his feet cradling me to his chest. It took both an eternity and an instant before he had us in a privacy room and I was on my feet and backed against the wall.

"Is this what you want?" Asher growled and yanked my dress up around my hips. "This?" he asked and hastily shoved my panties to the side before he thrust two fingers deep into me.

"Yes."

"Then take it." His voice vibrated with anger but I ignored it as I ground down on his fingers. "But when you come, you do it just for me."

Asher's intrusion felt violent as he fucked me with his fingers—curling and twisting before he pulled out and shoved them back in. I wrapped my arms around his shoulders, praying my legs wouldn't give out as my orgasm fast approached.

"Kiss me," I begged.

"Oh, no," he cruelly denied. "I warned you I didn't share. Not your body. Not your moans. And I sure as fuck don't share your orgasms. You pushed for this, now you take what I'm willing to give you. You wanna get off, take it, Sloane, but I will not kiss you. Not fucking here, not fucking ever in this goddamned place."

My body gave into his ministrations and the orgasm broke before I could process what he said or the disgust in his tone.

"Ash—"

"*No.*" His free hand hooked me around the back of the neck and he yanked me to his chest as my body betrayed me and continued to spasm around his fingers.

What did I just do?

Holy shit, what had I done?

"Oh my God," I mumbled against his suit jacket. "That wasn't..."

I trailed off, unable to vocalize my explanation. Not because I didn't know what happened, I did and it had not one thing to do with us being in a viewing room. I couldn't speak because shame bathed my skin and coated my insides. I was beyond embarrassed. I wasn't even humiliated—I was deeply horrified.

Asher had made it very, *very* clear he didn't want me. Yet I threw myself at him and took advantage of the situation.

Oh. My. God.

"I need to leave," I murmured.

Asher slowly withdrew his fingers and tugged down my dress. Okay, that was embarrassing.

"Sloane—"

"I'm sorry. So, so, sorry. That was wrong of me. So wrong I don't know what to say."

"Sweetness—"

What the fuck did I do?

I lifted my head and yanked myself out of Asher's hold.

"I don't feel good," I announced loudly, hoping there were cameras in the room. I needed this to be believable just in case Lorenzo or Will were watching. "I haven't eaten today and earlier I was woozy. Now my head is pounding. I feel a migraine coming on."

Asher's eyes narrowed knowing damn well I was lying but not able to call me on it or discuss what happened.

"I really need to get home before it hits," I carried on. "I need to find Mr. Kelly and tell him I'm going home."

"I'll walk you to your car."

"No," I rushed out. "I mean, there's no need."

"Sloane," he seethed. "I'm walking you to your car. Then I'll find Mr. Kelly and explain why you've left."

"That's—"

"End of." Asher's tone brokered no room for argument and really I just wanted to leave and never come back.

I'd fucked everything up.

Every. Thing.

Elise would be so disappointed in me.

"Okay," I gave in ungraciously and straightened my dress. "I need to grab my purse from the staff lounge."

With a jerk of his clenched jaw, Asher motioned for me to precede him. I had never in my life done a walk of shame so I couldn't know for sure, however, making my way through the great room of the mansion with Asher on my heels felt worse than any walk out of a man's house with yesterday's clothes on. I would swear I felt all eyes on me, burning into me, knowing what I'd done. Knowing I'd taken something from Asher he didn't want to give.

So much for the club's golden rule of consent.

"Mr. Newcomb," Lorenzo called out.

Could I not catch a break?

Could I not just get my purse and run away like a coward? Now I had to face Lorenzo, too. How had I allowed this to become my damn life?

"Sloane's ill, I'm going to walk her to her car," Asher returned.

"Sloane?"

Shit.

I wasn't sure if Lorenzo was requesting that I turn and look at him or if he found it odd that Asher was using my first name.

Boss up, Sloane, and face your executioner.

So, that was a little dramatic, but if he caught on to what I'd heard, he'd kill me, so maybe it wasn't.

Instead of turning fully I looked over my shoulder and made my apologies, which seemed to be the theme of the evening. Me, apologizing profusely to every man I'd come in contact with.

"Mr. Kelly, I'm sorry but I'm not feeling well. It started earlier, and well, I got dizzy and dropped a box of tumblers." *Shit, I forgot to restock them in the VIP room.* "Now I have a massive headache coming on."

"Perhaps you'd better lie down in one of the rooms," Lorenzo returned. "It's unwise for you to drive in your condition."

My condition wasn't ever something that would go away—I would forever be haunted by my selfishness and indecency.

"I appreciate your concern, but I'll be fine until I make it home."

Lorenzo bowed his head like he was some sort of gentleman bidding me a good night.

Sick bastard.

"Very well. I hope you feel better." Lorenzo's attention went from me to Asher. "Mr. Newcomb, we'll meet when you get back."

Wait, they'd meet?

Wordlessly, Asher grabbed my elbow. The silence stretched as he led me out of the mansion to my car.

"Keys," he demanded.

I quickly fished them out of my purse, wanting to make this as painless as possible. Unfortunately, Asher had other ideas and made them clear when he swung me around until my back was against my car and he was in my space.

"A few things," he rapped out and when he leaned in close, I held my breath for his wrath. "You go directly to the beach house. When you get there, tell Wilson there are ten VIPs here with three guards."

"What?"

"I have a meeting with Lorenzo when I get back in there. Tell that to Wilson, too. He'll know what it means. And tell him if I don't check in shit's gone sideways. Got that?"

Shit's gone sideways?

My heart rate picked up and those fake dizzy spells were becoming very real.

"What?"

"Sweetness, I need you to listen close. I need to get back in there. Ten VIPs, three guards, if I miss check-in, tell him to come get me."

Again, how was this happening? I was not made for this

kind of life. I'd always thought I wanted excitement and fireworks and thunder and lightning. Now I knew better. I wanted boring, the kind of mind-numbing tediousness that meant nothing dangerous would ever happen.

"Ash...Adam," I breathed past the lump in my throat. "Come with me. Right now, don't go back in there."

"And tonight, when I get home, we're talking about what happened and why you shut down on me."

I didn't want to have that conversation—as in ever.

But still...

"Come to the beach house with me and we'll talk about it right now."

"Hey, baby, hey." Both hands came up to cup my jaw and tilt my head back. "Everything's gonna be okay."

No, I didn't think it would be okay. Asher was going back into the lion's den and he didn't know what he was up against.

"You don't know what I heard. Will Evans was talking to another man about getting another girl. One that will not be missed like the last one. And they were arguing about Sammy. I didn't see the other guy, but he wanted to take her *tonight*. Will said no because she lived with her dad."

Asher's expression was set straight to pissed-the-fuck-off and his eyes had grown hard.

"Straight to the beach house, Sloane. When you get there, tell Wilson. He'll know what to do and he'll keep you safe until I get home."

I would've asked if I was in danger but that was a stupid freaking question. At least Asher didn't add salt to the wound by reminding me he'd told me to quit this afternoon.

"I have to get back in there," he reminded me.

"Please..." I paused to calm my nerves but after a few seconds I gave up the notion. Nothing was going to calm my worry until this night was over and Asher was home safe. "Promise you'll be careful."

"Nothing to worry about, sweetness."

"That's not a promise."

"Promise."

"You promise you'll come home tonight?" I finally asked the question I really wanted to know.

Everything about Asher softened before he leaned down and brushed his lips over mine. It was there he uttered his assurance.

"Promise."

When Asher backed away my hand lifted and I pressed my fingers to my lips. It wasn't until I pulled into the driveway of the beach house that I realized I'd driven there one-handed, too afraid to let go of Asher's promise.

17

"WHO'S THIS?" I motioned to the man sitting in front of Lorenzo's desk in one of the two black leather chairs.

"Who he is for the purpose of this meeting is the man who can get you what you need," Lorenzo shot back, smiling.

Smug prick.

"And Will? What's he doing here?"

It was time to drop the formalities—there was no respect among us and continuing to pretend there was, was a waste of time.

"He, too, can get you what you need."

Interesting. It would seem Lorenzo was the middleman, not the mastermind.

"I have no idea what you're talking about, Lorenzo."

"Don't be foolish."

"This is not how I do business."

I turned toward the door but halted when Will spoke. "We don't do holds or layaways, *Adam*. You either take possession of the merchandise when it becomes available, or you lose your spot."

Fuck.

I took in the man sitting silently in the chair. I'd bet the second voice Sloane heard belonged to him.

I had no choice but to play.

"When will it be available?"

Will smirked and instinctively I knew to brace.

"Won't be long. In the interim, you got yourself a sweet piece of ass to keep you occupied. I have to admit, I didn't think she had it in her." Will smiled at me with a dare. "Would've fucked her a long time ago if I knew she lit up like that. Bitch hides it well—all prim and proper-like—until you got her on your lap. I was disappointed, thought for sure she was gonna drop to her knees and suck you off."

My temper flared and anger shafted through me in fast, burning pulses.

"You interested in seeing my cock?" I sneered.

"Only with her lips wrapped around it."

Sick motherfucking bastard.

I held his stare, making a silent vow to break his neck when this was over.

"I'm leaving tomorrow on a business trip. I won't be back for a week. If the merchandise is secured before then, you will hold it for me until I return. I want it untouched. No bruising. I hate marks that I haven't made myself and I don't want to wait until they fade."

"That's not how this works," Will informed me.

"This is the only way it's gonna work. I don't know you and I don't know him." I jabbed a finger at the man still sitting. "I already told you this is not the way I do business. But you have something I want, so I'll make a few concessions. But hear this, Will, you fuck me over on this deal, I'll see to it you're put out of business *permanently.*"

"You've got some big balls coming—"

"I think what you mean to say is I've got a big dick, and you'd be right. You think you've got the upper hand with me coming into this meeting blind, but you have no idea."

"What'd you say?" Will asked, doing his best to be threatening.

"I said I'd be back in a week to pick up the goods."

Needing to end the conversation before I snapped Will's neck, I walked to the door but stopped short of turning the knob. Looking at Lorenzo, I followed my hunch.

"I want that video deleted, Lorenzo. I find out you didn't erase it, you got problems."

Being the shit criminal Lorenzo was, he couldn't stop his cheek muscle from jumping.

He also didn't deny there were cameras in the privacy rooms. Motherfucker was recording members without their consent. Either he got off knowing he was invading their privacy, or he was using the recordings as blackmail. Probably both.

"Call me when you have what I want."

With that I left Lorenzo's office, scanning the main room as I made my way back to Dee to get my phone and check out. The VIPs were nowhere in sight, and neither were the bodyguards. Sammy was likely entertaining them in the dungeon downstairs. A room that was not on the blueprints of the mansion. Which begged the question—how many other secret rooms were there and what were they used for?

———

I HADN'T EVEN TURNED the engine off when the front door to the beach house swung open, and Sloane appeared looking like the temptress she was in nothing but one of my t-shirts. Thankfully it hit mid-thigh. Also thankfully my jealousy had taken a hiatus because I didn't contemplate Cole's murder when he stepped behind her, hooked her around the waist, and yanked her back inside.

I shut down the BMW, stepped out, and prepared myself for the battle that would surely ensue once I told Sloane my plan. The woman was going to be unhappy, as in furious. My only hope was that tonight freaked her out enough to make her understand the danger she was in was real. She wasn't starring in an episode of Scooby-Doo where the bad guy was an old man, Mr. Charlie dressed up like the Grinch to stop trick or treaters from knocking on his door. Lorenzo was not going to go down quietly. Will Evans wasn't going to take his punishment like a man. Neither was asshole number three. And those were the ones I knew about. Until this was over, Sloane was going to Idaho.

But first, we had things to discuss—top of that list was the shit she pulled tonight. There had been times in both my careers in law enforcement when I had to make tough calls that I sometimes second-guessed, but any decision I'd made had been necessary for the safety of those around me and for the operational integrity of the investigation. But not tonight. All rational thought fled, and selfishness guided my decisions. Selfishness *and* anger. The infinite amount of determination it had taken not fuck Sloane in the privacy room was only fueled by my suspicion the rooms were wired for video. That and my disgust for the mansion in general, though in that moment with Sloane pressed up against me, her face soft, her thoughts dirty and body willing, I wasn't thinking about the mansion or the reasons why I couldn't allow myself to have her—my control had snapped on that. It was the thought of me fucking her being captured on video that had stopped me.

"You're home early."

The relief in Sloane's voice registered and instead of appreciating her concern, it pissed me off.

"We need to talk," I declared like an asshole. "We'll be out in a minute."

On my way past Sloane, I tagged her hand and jerked her into motion. I didn't use the time it took to get to my bedroom to calm down. I didn't think about the consequences of my next move or the aftermath, or the destruction they would cause. I allowed all my pent-up emotions to get the best of me and as soon as we entered the room, I threw the door shut and slammed my mouth on hers.

Without hesitation, Sloane opened hers and shoved her tongue past my lips. Every fucking swipe, every stroke, every lick wrought an unquenchable need. The kiss built until Sloane's hands were ripping at my shirt and my hands were on her lace-covered ass cheeks.

This was where it should've ended. I'd been hanging onto my resolve by the barest of threads, knowing having her would only prolong the ache in my chest when I was gone. But that thread had snapped. There was no more holding out, there was no more denying Sloane was my fate —either to have or to mourn—but she was *mine*.

All fucking mine.

By the time the back of her legs hit the bed she'd untucked my shirt and her hands were roaming my back. I toed off my shoes, broke the kiss, and looked into her lusty eyes.

"You sure?"

"Yes."

"I need you to be sure."

She blinked some of the fog away and nodded.

"You're gonna ruin me," she whispered.

"No, baby, I'm gonna ruin us," I corrected and began unbuttoning my shirt.

Sloane's hands slid over my ribs and then down until they were working my belt. To further communicate she was on board with our demise, she leaned forward and pressed a kiss to my chest. She waited for another button to open, and she pressed another kiss there. Then another and another until all the buttons were undone and her mouth was at my navel.

Her beautiful eyes tipped up and collided with mine, making me question everything. How the fuck was I going to walk away? I now understood Rhode. He'd been willing to give up his job to be a part of his son's life, but for Brooklyn, he was willing to give up everything. There was nothing he wouldn't give or do to keep her.

Sloane slipped her fingers into the waistband of my boxers and pulled me from my thoughts as she worked the material over my erection. Her eyes flared as she wrapped a hand around my cock, giving me a firm, slow stroke.

"Baby," I groaned.

Her thumb grazed the tip and circled it. On a downward glide, she whispered, "Ruin me, Asher."

Fuck.

"Sloane—"

"I'm yours to ruin."

Jesus.

She had no idea what she was saying—no idea the beast she'd awoken. An uncivilized part of me, a need to claim, to mark, to own her body and soul, to ruin her for all other men. To make her crave only me. The other edge of that particular sword was I wanted to be hers, I wanted her to mark *me*, own *me*, claim *me*. I wanted her to want to give up everything to have me.

"Let go."

My demand came out harsher than I'd intended. Not that Sloane minded. The temptress didn't let go—she bent forward and sucked the head of my cock into her mouth. Her tongue rolled around the sensitive indentation just below the tip.

"Sloane." Her name came out as a groan through my gritted teeth as I held myself back from thrusting into her mouth.

She pulled her mouth off my cock. She tipped her eyes up but my focus was on the wet tip resting on her bottom lip, the sight so fucking hot it wouldn't have taken more than a few strokes of her hand before I painted those lips with my come.

Incapable of forming a coherent sentence, I barked my orders while I shrugged off my shirt. "Up. Panties off. Bed."

Sloane scrambled to do my bidding while I finished taking off the rest of my clothes. By the time I straightened she was in the middle of the bed, my t-shirt around her waist, bare pussy on display.

"Leave my shirt on but pull it up. I wanna see all of you."

I watched as she slowly pulled the fabric up over her breasts. My eyes narrowed and shot to hers.

"New rule," I rapped out. "Bra stays on when my friends are over."

She smirked and lowered her hands to cup her breasts, pushing them together in a tease.

"I would've, but I wasn't wearing a bra under my dress."

I didn't dwell on the thought of her braless under her tight dresses. After tonight, she'd never set foot back into the mansion.

"Keep your hands where they are and spread your legs for me."

"Bossy," she muttered but followed my instructions.

I wasn't bossy, I was a take-sex-as-it-came kind of guy. I'd never commanded a partner in bed, I'd never made demands, but Sloane was different. I'd known that from the beginning and seeing as the need to dominate her pulsed through me with an indecent beat I couldn't ignore, only strengthened the knowledge.

"Wider, Sloane, I wanna see how wet you are."

Her legs opened wider, and I took her in—from her pussy to her hands still cupping her full tits to her eyes staring at me with anticipation.

"You... are... so... *fucking*... beautiful."

I climbed on the bed, pausing to kiss the inside of each thigh. And since I'd been waiting, I dipped between her legs, and with a single swipe of my tongue from ass to clit I finally tasted her.

"Asher," she moaned, and I lifted my head.

"Say it again."

"Asher."

There it was, my fucking name. Not Adam. Mine.

And hearing it incited my need. I hooked her leg under my arm and surged up, taking it with me and opening her further. I planted my elbow in the bed next to her shoulder.

"Guide me in."

Both her hands fell away from her breasts. One went between us, the other gripped my shoulder, and she guided me home.

With a single thrust, we were fully connected. Sloane's back arched off the mattress and her nails scored a path down my spine while a low groan emanated from her chest.

Jesus Christ.

Suddenly reality invaded.

"Condom," I grunted.

"No need, I'm covered."

Fuck.

"Sweetness—"

"IUD."

I kept myself still, fighting the urge to take her while mentally kicking my own ass for not thinking about this before I felt her wet heat pulsing around my cock.

"You sure?"

"Positive."

To affirm her acquiescence Sloane wrapped her legs around my waist and lifted her hips.

There was no going slow. The world slipped away and all that was left was Sloane's soft body, slick pussy, and the sounds of her breath leaving her lungs with every hard, pounding drive. I was beyond finesse, beyond control, beyond lust. Need drove my cock deep—the need to hear her call out *my* name as she climaxed. The need to feel her shake and tremble. The need to challenge her to deny we were meant to be.

"Ash—" she puffed out on a breath.

"Tighter, sweetness, hold on."

Her ankles locked and her hands roamed my back, alternating between nails scratching and palms gliding. Her eyes were wide with something that looked like wonder and I was positive mine were the same. But it was the sweet, serene smile tugging at her lips that did me in. She was just as close as I was. Teetering on the edge of pleasure and ecstasy. The blissed-out place that felt so fucking good you did your best to fall over the cliff. But I wanted to fall with Sloane. I wanted to feel her clench around me. I wanted her orgasm to coat my cock while mine bathed her cunt.

And I wanted that with a desperate desire, and I wanted it now.

Right. Fucking. *Now.*

I balanced on my forearm, shoved my free hand under her head, grabbed a fistful of hair, and dropped my mouth to hers.

"Come with me, Sloane," I demanded and ground down. "Right now, sweetness."

On a downward thrust Sloane bucked, her pussy clamped tight, and as the moan slipped past her lips I took her mouth. Two more thrusts and I joined her. Two more after that the pleasure became unbearable and I stayed planted as Sloane's orgasm pulsed around me, pulling what felt like unending ropes of pleasure from my body.

Jesus.

Christ.

After what seemed like forever the tension in my neck loosened but Sloane's limbs wrapped around me did not. She was holding me tight and, in a place reserved only for her, I found a sick joy in the knowledge she was holding me close—not letting go of me.

But as all good things must come to an end, it was time to face what I'd allowed.

A reckoning of sorts.

I knew what connecting with Sloane would mean. With my cock still wet from our combined orgasms, my chest was burning with the loss of her. A loss that hadn't happened yet but would soon enough. The deep understanding that I'd tasted something beautiful, but it would never be mine to keep.

"You're coming to Idaho with me," I declared without preamble.

Sloane's legs tightened but the rest of her body went solid.

"What?"

"We're leaving tonight," I continued to inform her.

"Tonight?"

"Tonight."

"Why?"

Because I never want to be without you and I'm going to use this time as a way to persuade you to stay with me.

"You're not safe here."

Her limbs released me, and I instantly felt the sting of disappointment.

"Right."

"Sloane—"

"You don't have to convince me. I know after what I overheard tonight, I'm in danger."

I should've felt relief she was going to go without an argument, and it was irrational of me to be pissed at her because I'd been a coward and not told her the truth. But I wanted her to call me on my bullshit. I wanted her to ask me if that was the only reason I was taking her home with me.

"We need to talk about what happened at the club tonight." No sooner did the words leave my mouth than Sloane was wiggling to get free.

"Get off me."

I flexed my hips keeping my softening cock inside her and denied her request.

"Nope. We talk like this."

"Why? I want to get dressed."

I didn't bother reminding her that dressed was merely rolling my tee back down from under her neck where it was still gathered. I also wasn't going to dwell on how much I liked seeing her in my tee or how much I liked the feel of her tits pressed against my chest.

"I need to understand what happened earlier and I need you to understand why I didn't kiss you."

Her eyes went over my shoulder and she shook her head.

"Get—"

"Baby, look at me." I waited until her gaze drifted back.

The dejection I saw in her eyes fucking killed.

"I couldn't," I started. "I was so close to losing control I couldn't kiss you. You were lost in the moment, and I knew when you came back to your senses, you'd be angry—at me and at yourself. I was fucking stuck, Sloane. I wanted to give you what you wanted but my need to protect you weighed out."

Some of the sadness slid out of her eyes only to be replaced by a blank expression.

"Your turn," I prompted when she didn't speak.

"Thank you."

My eyes narrowed and I jerked back. "That's it?"

"Well, yeah, thank you for knowing I'd be angry at—"

"I don't want your gratitude, I want you to explain to me how we got there."

"Got there?"

Jesus, I was fast losing my hold on my irritation.

"Yeah, Sloane, how'd we get from you sitting on my lap in the viewing room to me finger-fucking you in a privacy room? Was it Jacob eating—"

"No," she snapped. "It had nothing to do with the show. I promise."

"Then I need you to explain it to me. I was careful not to touch you. Hell, I was thinking of a thousand things to keep my mind occupied so I wouldn't think of you in my lap in that short-ass excuse of a dress you were wearing."

Maybe that was why when I saw her in my t-shirt waiting for me at the door I felt relief instead of jealousy. My shirt was longer and baggier than the form-fitting cocktail dress she'd worn to work.

Yeah, that was bullshit, but I was going with that instead of admitting I was a knuckle-dragging caveman who liked seeing her in my tee and what that said to my friends.

"There's nothing wrong with my dress," she shot back.

"We're not talking about the dress. We're talking about the lengths I went to so my dick wouldn't get hard under your ass with you wiggling around and the wrong conclusions you could draw from that."

"I told you, it wasn't the show. At least not entirely."

What the fuck?

"What's that mean?"

I didn't know why I was pressing the issue so hard. There wasn't a damn thing wrong with getting hot from watching porn—whether it be live or on a screen. But I had to know if it was her being close to me or if it was Jacob eating his woman's pussy in front of her that turned her on.

Sloane blew out a stuttered breath. And suddenly I didn't want to know, not when I watched the embarrassment wash over her.

"Sweetness—"

"I was jealous," she admitted, and I felt every muscle in my body contract. "I mean, not because of Jacob. I was jealous of her...I mean, jealous of what she was feeling." Sloane trailed off and when she stammered out the rest of her explanation my body got tighter and tighter. "She sounded like she was in the throes of a pleasure I'd never known. I was jealous of that. Then you licked my neck and put your hand on my throat and suddenly I could no longer hear the moans or see what was happening in front of me. All of my attention was on your hand wrapped around my throat and how much I liked it there. Then you told me, in another place and time you'd have my dress around my hips and my mind wandered to that place. And I guess I got carried away in my fantasy. But it wasn't the show, it was you. I'm sorry, Asher. I know—"

"You don't know," I cut her off. "You have no fucking idea how hard it's gonna be to watch you walk away from me."

"I do know," she whispered. "We're ruined."

No truer words had ever been spoken.

"Yeah, baby, we are."

I pulled out and rolled to the side, angry as fuck I'd given in.

My eyes greedily swept over her naked body before I leaned over and kissed her forehead, then exited the bed and walked across the room.

"Asher," she called.

"Yeah?"

"I take it back," she said to my back. "I'm not sorry. You might be but I'd rather have what we shared just once than never have it all."

I remained frozen. Sloane however did not. I heard her footsteps approach and I braced for a touch that never came. Though the sight of her in my tee as she walked past me into the bathroom was just as, if not more, effective.

Fucking hell, I was screwed.

18

I WAS STILL in Asher's shirt when I walked out into the living room. I'd given myself a pep talk while I cleaned up. Well, it was actually a suck-it-up-and-be-a-big-girl talk. And part of that talk was to remind myself I was a grown-ass woman, and it was perfectly acceptable for me to have sex and it did not make me a slut—even if the other occupants, who happen to be men heard. Another part of my talk was to prepare myself for any looks or comments directed at me by Wilson or Cole. And the final part was to resign myself to the fact I needed Asher's protection and I wasn't going to argue. So, it wasn't so much of a talk as it was a short chat.

I'd spent the rest of the time mildly annoyed that I had finally experienced ten out of ten sex and Asher ruined it by bringing up what happened at the club. I knew we needed to discuss it, but he'd screwed up my afterglow. Something I'd never experienced and was luxuriating in until he started talking.

Cole lifted his gaze from his laptop when I entered the dining room. After careful consideration, I decided he wasn't looking at me any differently than he did before Asher got home.

"So, you think they'll wait?" I heard Wilson ask. I'd obviously come in on the middle of a conversation so I waited to see who he was speaking to.

"I think Lorenzo's a fucking idiot and Will isn't too far behind," Asher replied.

"That's not an answer."

"It might not be the answer you want but the truth will piss you off more so it's the only one I'm gonna give you."

"You don't care—"

"Oh, I fucking care," Asher interrupted. "I want Will Evans put down. I want Lorenzo's ass in jail and I want to find and rescue the girls they have. I want Elise found. And I want Samantha Price clear of the club. But right now, my concern is getting Sloane safe. After that, I'll come back."

Right now, my concern is getting Slone safe.

I stopped mid-stride and stared at the back of Asher's head.

He wanted me safe.

If I hadn't given my heart to Asher sometime in the last twenty-four hours, I was sure it would've been beating out of my chest. But all the shriveled-up organ was doing was dying more.

"What if I just hid here?" I suggested. "Then you wouldn't have to wait."

"No." Asher turned in the chair and any further protests died in my dry throat. "Lorenzo knows I'm into you. He made a point of mentioning it. Not that he came straight out and said it, but he knew I was looking for you and lied to me. He told me you weren't there—he did that to get a reaction. When we were done with our conversation, he told me you were downstairs, again to see how I'd react.

But even if he hadn't caught on to me watching you at the club, he has cameras, which means after tonight he knows unequivocally that I'm into you after months of me being there and turning down every woman who's propositioned me."

Jealousy prickled as it pierced my skin.

Before I could comment he continued, "Then there's Will Evans and his sidekick, who spent the ten minutes I was in Lorenzo's office arguing with the two dirtbags about arranging the purchase of a human, completely mute. I don't like silence. I get the feeling Will's the man in charge, or he works for him and Lorenzo's the broker. What that means is Will's smart and it's only a matter of time before he digs into you and finds your connection with Elise. Before that happens, I want you up in Idaho where I can protect you. If the deal goes south, then we find another way to take them down. We know enough now, we don't need the sale to go through. It'd be faster, but we don't need it."

"Okay."

"Okay?" Asher repeated.

"Yes, I'm not going to argue about this." I sucked in a breath in preparation to eat crow. "You were right, I should've quit this afternoon on the phone. Though, a tiny part of me is happy I didn't because I heard Will and I know he took Elise. And while we're on the topic of overhearing conversations, what about Sammy? Will said he didn't want her but what if they get impatient and change their minds?"

Wilson was quick to field my question. "I already called my contact at the Marshals, they're contacting local authorities and she'll be under constant surveillance. If they make a move on her, they'll be taken in."

"Thank you," I whispered.

"No need to thank me, Sloane. This is what we do."

I guessed it was, but I was still relieved someone would be watching out for Sammy.

My attention went back to Asher and, serious as shit, my breath caught in my throat. I glanced back at Wilson, then to Cole, before going back to Asher. I'd prepared myself for the possible looks the other men would give me, the reprimand or disapproval but I hadn't been prepared for Asher.

He was staring at me somewhere between soft and sweet and knowingly and lustfully.

Belatedly it hit me, really hit me—I had sex with Asher.

Really great sex.

I'd seen him naked—gloriously naked. All his hard muscles and smooth skin. My palms had traveled his back, my hands had squeezed his firm ass, my legs had wrapped around his trim waist. My only regret was that in my haste to feel him inside of me, I hadn't had the chance to explore all the goodness that was Asher with my lips and tongue.

"Sloane?" Asher called.

"Huh?"

"Baby, we're leaving in ten minutes."

That jerked me out of my fog.

"Okay." Then a thought hit me. "How long do you think I'll be gone? I don't have a suitcase. I mean, I have a carry-on but that's all."

Asher studied me, and as he did, the sweetness slid out of his features and his expression turned blank.

"We're going straight to the airport from here."

"But I'll need clothes."

"I'll buy you clothes in Idaho."

That was nice of Asher to offer but it wasn't going to happen. I could buy my own clothes.

"I also need—"

"Sloane, whatever you need, we'll get in Idaho. We're not taking the chance of going to your place then being followed."

That made sense but still, I wanted some of my stuff.

"You're taking this well," Cole noted and closed his laptop. "I figured there'd be at least some sort of drama. Letty would've been throwing a hissy fit right now."

I had no idea who Letty was but the way that Asher smiled upon hearing the woman's name made me instantly not like her.

When had I become so catty?

"Yeah, well, I'm not Letty," I snapped. "And I've seen enough movies to know what happens to the innocent woman who accidentally hears something she shouldn't've. I'm not trying to be a two-part miniseries. I'm not stupid enough to turn down protection even if it means giving up my life for a little while. It's not like I have anything tying me to California at the moment. And until Elise comes home, I'm more than happy not to be in my lonely apartment. Everything in there is a reminder my friend isn't home."

Actually, every time I stepped foot into my apartment it was torture. All I could think about were the horrors Elise must've been going through.

I would've moved but the apartment was Elise's home, too. And I couldn't bring myself to pack up her belongings. In my mind that was like admitting Elise wasn't coming home and I couldn't do that. I had to have hope. I had to believe my friend was out there waiting for me to find her.

"No, you're not Letty," Cole unnecessarily confirmed. "Thank God for that. I love that woman, but damn can she turn any situation into drama."

If the way Cole was smiling was any indication, he was telling the truth. Wilson was also sporting a small grin, which was out of character for the man. I chanced a glance at Asher and braced for his smile but he was still expressionless.

What was that about?

The guy gave me whiplash with his hot and cold. He wanted me, then he didn't. But more, he made me feel wanted. He straight out told me how he felt but then slammed the door closed on the topic like it was a given we had no chance. Which meant he really didn't want me because if he did, he'd find a way. He lived in Idaho, not Pluto. There were these things called planes and cars and phones, and people did long-distance relationships all the time. So really it was all bullshit, he didn't feel what I felt.

But what wasn't bullshit was that sex with Asher had ruined me. From this point on he would forever be the gold standard. So maybe I didn't regret only having one chance to explore his body. Maybe it was a good thing he hadn't taken the time to explore mine. But I knew that was wrong, it wasn't the sex—though it was good—it was Asher. The way he'd looked at me while moving inside of me like he'd been searching for me his whole life and he was amazed he'd found me. Or maybe I was projecting because he was the man I'd been searching for. The long shot, the one-in-a-million kind of love that takes you by surprise. The kind that even if you tried you couldn't fend it off.

So, yes, I was forever ruined by Asher.

He'd leave, or actually, he'd send me home and he'd stay in Idaho, and he'd make no move to ask me to stay. And the fuck of it was, if he asked, I'd move. I would have to wait until after I found Elise and I had her settled. But after that, I'd leave my life in California.

When I could take no more of Asher's blank-face stare I rudely blurted, "Are we leaving or what?"

"Maybe she does have a little drama in her," Cole started, and I transferred my dirty look to him. "Oh, yeah, you're fucked, brother. My advice is to keep her away from Letty, it wouldn't take much coaching before Sloane here learns how to throw a Letty-sized tantrum. One of her in the group is more than enough. Call Sadie and ask her around instead. The woman's sweet down to her soul, maybe she'll rub off on your woman."

Your woman?

What the hell and who was Sadie?

"Are you saying I'm not sweet?" I inquired.

"I'm not stupid enough to answer that."

"That is an answer, Cole. When have I not been sweet to you?"

"Right now?"

Cole's question came about with a smile unlike any of the others I'd seen. This one was playful, teasing, almost boyish, which was ridiculous because Cole was a man—all man. But the proof he could be playful was right in front of me and it looked damn good on him. Now, if Wilson would loosen up a bit and maybe smile, I wouldn't be so wary of him. However, he seemed to have a distrustful disposition.

"Right now, I'm not throwing drama, I'm in the middle of a drama," I educated him.

Cole chuckled and nodded a few times before he said, "Ah, okay, I see the difference."

He didn't. But in the interest of saving time and not proving his point by continuing the conversation, I hotly announced, "I'm going to go change."

I turned on my heels and flounced through the living

room only to stop at the mouth of the hall when I heard Wilson.

"Not sure what I'm more impressed by, her holding her own in that club or that exit. I'd say you're fucked, brother, but you already know you are. So instead I'll tell you—let her walk, you're a damn fool."

I'd impressed Wilson. He thought Asher would be a fool if he let me go.

Holy shit.

Holy. Shit.

It took me a moment to catch my breath and get my wits about me before I finished walking down the hall into Asher's room. I made the trek with a smile on my face, maybe Wilson liked me after all.

19

BY THE TIME we landed in Idaho, it was nearing on four in the morning. One of the many benefits of flying on a private jet was scheduling—the plane left when you got there and not before. The other benefit was we didn't need to fly to Spokane International and make the drive to Coeur d'Alene. There was a small municipal airport in the heart of Kootenai County. In recent years it had seen its fair share of traffic with all the celebrities flying in and out. CDA was no longer Idaho's best-kept secret; it was becoming the premier vacation spot both in the summer and winter. Something I'd heard the locals complain about, not that I blamed them. We were all outsiders invading their home.

Though I had to admit, while I understood the locals I didn't feel an ounce of remorse about moving to Idaho. There was something about being surrounded by the lakes and mountains that fed the soul. Being tucked away and surrounded by the beauty of the forest brought me a peace I never found in the city. I was happy to leave Arizona when Wilson relocated our headquarters. I was more than happy to leave the heat and the fast pace of life. Until I moved to

Idaho, I hadn't known I needed the calm and quiet. I'd been nearing burnout after so many years in law enforcement. All the shit I'd seen and investigated had caught up with me in the form of night terrors and borderline paranoia. After I'd gotten to Idaho it had taken less than a month for the nightmares to go away.

"See you later?" Cole asked as the steward opened the door of the jet for debarkation.

Sloane stirred next to me and lifted her head off my shoulder. She'd fallen asleep on the drive to Santa Barbara, woken up briefly to board the plane, looked around the cabin, then took a seat and was back asleep before we were airborne.

"Are we here?"

Her sleepy voice hit me the same way it did the morning I'd woken up with her curled up next to me in her bed, but with the added benefit of knowing how she tasted, felt, and sounded like when she came around my cock. And since all logical thought had abandoned me and had yet to return, I was thinking about how the next time Sloane woke up next to me, she would not be in one of her fancy dresses, she'd be naked. After I took my time with her.

"Yeah, baby, we're here."

"Why do you do that?" Her question came out on a yawn and she quickly covered her mouth. "Sorry. Yucky morning breath."

Fuck, she was cute.

"Why do I do what?"

"Sometimes you call me baby, but sometimes you call me sweetness."

That was not an explanation I wanted to give, but I knew Sloane and she'd push it until I came clean.

"Sometimes, sweetness still slips out. Sometimes, I plain

forget. But when I remember or I'm thinking about it I call you baby because Lorenzo told me his fresh girls taste like sweetness."

Sloane jerked upright. Her nose was adorably scrunched, and her lips were pinched tightly together until she opened them to squeak, "Gross!"

"That sums it up nicely."

"I don't think I like you calling me sweetness anymore. Which sucks because I used to like it. Yet another reason to hate Lorenzo," she confessed.

I vaguely wondered if she hadn't been still half-asleep if she would've admitted to liking me calling her sweetness. I also wondered how after the night we'd had, and how I'd behaved like a dick after I fucked her, how she could still want to be close to me. There were plenty of empty seats on the private jet with only three people flying. She could've picked one far away from mine. But she'd plopped down next to me and rested her head on my shoulder.

"Yo!" Cole called from the front of the plane, reminding me I'd yet to answer him.

"Yeah, we'll be in the office this afternoon. You text Wilson and tell him we landed?"

"Yep."

Cole took his leave and Sloane stood. I was immediately assaulted by her long, tanned legs before she bent in front of me to pick up the heels she'd kicked off sometime during the flight. Her head turned to the side and her eyes widened.

"Sorry."

She immediately straightened and tugged on the hem of her dress, but it was too late. I'd already gotten an eye full of ass cheek.

"Are you, 'cause I'm not," I told her honestly.

She gave me a sleepy grin and shook her head. "Stop

teasing me when I'm too tired to form a proper comeback."

"I wasn't teasing. I've had your ass in my hands a few times now but I've yet to get a good view."

Her smile faded, her brows pulled together, and she frowned.

"And whose fault is that?"

"Mine. Entirely mine," I conceded.

What I didn't tell her was I was going to rectify that oversight as quickly as I could.

Since the door had been opened and the damage done, I'd decided we were going to enjoy each other as much as we could. I was going to gorge on every inch of her until our time was up. And if I was lucky, when the time came, she wouldn't want to leave. I wasn't stupid enough to think sex alone would get her to stay. I was willing to do anything—I'd tie myself in knots until I convinced her to take a chance on me.

I was starting with orgasms but then I'd give her something she couldn't get in California—a family. I wouldn't have to do anything but introduce her to Brooklyn, Letty, and Sadie. From there they'd do the rest. Those women were pathologically friendly. They'd take one look at Sloane, listen to her story, and they'd pull her into the fold.

That was how I'd win her over.

That was how I'd get her to stay.

Because a life without Sloane wasn't an option.

———

"WOW, YOU...UM...LIVE HERE?"

Sloane's eyes went around the great room, taking in the sparsely furnished space. The sawhorses, the saws, nail gun, tarps, and paint cans.

I couldn't help the burst of laughter. She looked positively scandalized at the state of my unfinished downstairs.

"Why are you laughing at me?" she huffed.

"Bet you wish you would've asked where you were staying before you agreed to come to Idaho with me," I said, still chuckling.

"Take that back," she snapped, and a hand went to her hip.

The truth was I wasn't well-versed in all the ways a woman communicated her displeasure. However, some of the telltale signs were pretty obvious. The hand on the hip being a dead giveaway I'd pissed her off.

"Baby, I'm joking."

"I'm not stuck up."

"I know you're not. I was joking."

"So take it back."

Obviously, I'd misjudged the hand on the hip.

She wasn't pissed—she was *pissed*. As in flames were going to start shooting out of her eyeballs at any moment. Pissed in a way that meant I needed to sleep with one eye open if I didn't want to be a ball short of a pair in the morning.

"Okay, I'll take it back if you tell me what's wrong."

Her other hand came up and she raked her fingers through her hair.

"Shit. I'm sorry."

Both hands fell to her sides, but I wasn't dumb enough to think I was out of the woods. This seemed like one of those feminine ruses that lulled a man into a false sense of security, so I let my guard down.

But still, I asked, "Why are you sorry?"

"I'm tired and grouchy and I've had a shit day. I'm still freaked out about what I heard and Lorenzo setting up a meeting for you to buy a person. That's insane. Totally crazy. Who sells a person? What kind of person buys a human? I miss Elise like crazy. I miss her so much I've convinced myself she's coming home. I want to pick up the phone and call her. I want to text her and tell her about you. I want her to give me advice. I want to sit with her on our couch with a glass of wine and a bag of popcorn and tell her I finally had good sex. I want her to tell me I'm crazy for working at Club Joi and get mad at me for putting my life in danger. She'd be so pissed at me, she'd yell and cuss but then she'd forgive me because that's what best friends do."

She shook her head. "I hate our friends. I hate them all for turning their backs on me and abandoning me. I'm so tired I want to sleep for a week. This isn't my life and I don't want to live it anymore but saying that makes me the bitchiest bitch in the whole world because if I wasn't living it I wouldn't be trying to find Elise. And now I'm in Idaho not because *you* wanted to *invite* me to your house and show me..." She finally paused to take a breath and look around the room. "Show me this, whatever this project is. Nope. I'm in Idaho because it's too dangerous for me to be in California. And because of all that, I'm behaving like a child and demanding you take back a comment. And I'm happy Cole's not here to witness this because I'm pretty sure *this* is the definition of throwing drama."

This wasn't drama. This was everything piling on top of Sloane again.

"Two breakdowns in two days, you must think I'm a basket case."

I shrugged off my backpack, dropped it on the floor, and closed the distance between us.

"Come on, let's get you in the shower and then to bed."

Sloane eyed the room suspiciously before her exhausted

eyes came back to mine. It was the dead-on-her-feet look that made my decision easy. I swung her up into my arms into a fireman's hold and started across the living room.

"I can walk."

"You might step on a nail," I lied.

"I'm wearing shoes."

"You're wearing high heels and this is a construction zone," I told her and started climbing the stairs.

"Does that mean I need to wear a hard hat and one of those orange vests if I want to see your downstairs in the daylight?"

Suddenly a filthy vision of Sloane wearing nothing but a hard hat, caution vest, and a pair of work boots filled my mind.

"Tomorrow I'm buying a hard hat."

"Are you crazy?"

I was beginning to think I was, so I didn't bother answering.

I stepped into the master, flipped on the light, and heard Sloane suck in a breath. Unlike the rest of the house, the bedroom remodel was done. I'd blown out the wall to the room next door to add space for a walk-in closet and enlarged the bathroom. The vaulted ceiling now had knotty alder tongue and groove. The walls were painted stark white, but it was the stone fireplace I was most proud of.

"Did you do this?"

"Yep."

"Holy shit, Asher, this is amazing."

"Wait until you see the bathroom."

I skirted the bed, happy I'd changed the sheets before I left, and I walked into the bathroom.

"Flip the switch, baby."

Sloane reached out and tagged the lights. This time she

didn't inhale—she gasped, then she struggled until I set her on her feet.

"You did this, too?" she asked as she spun in a circle.

I was proud of the work I'd done in my bedroom, but the bathroom was next level.

Sloane walked to the shower and peeked her head in.

"You have four...no, six shower heads."

"Yep."

"Do you need six shower heads?"

Did I need them? No. Was I happy I had them? Fuck yes.

"Nope."

Sloane straightened and took in the granite double vanity then her gaze skidded to the oversize bathtub.

"Wanna take a bath?"

She continued to stare at the tub without answering me. As a matter of fact, she looked far away and lost.

"Sloane?"

Her head tilted to the side and that was when I saw a tear roll down her cheek.

"Yes, I want to take a bath. And yes I want to look around your awesome room and admire your work while you tell me everything you did and how you did it. And yes I want to take a shower and turn on all six shower heads. But I'm so exhausted I'm too tired."

"Then let's get you into bed."

"But I'm gross."

"Then let's get in the shower."

"I'm too—"

Since I didn't know where the hell the zipper to her dress was, I shut her up by reaching for the hem and yanking it up. Her arms went up, the dress cleared her head, and I tossed it on the floor.

"Kick off your shoes."

I didn't wait to see if she followed my orders. I moved to the shower, turned the tap to hot, and adjusted the handles until all the nozzles were spraying water. By the time I turned back around, Sloane was naked. I quickly toed out of my shoes and just as quickly shucked my clothes. Wordlessly, I led her into the huge walk-in shower.

"I'm sorry," she whispered.

"Listen to me." I pulled her under the rainfall spigot mounted on the ceiling. "You have nothing to be sorry for. Like you said, you've had a rough day and you're exhausted. Add to that you're someplace you've never been. Tomorrow will be better."

"Promise?"

"Yeah, baby, I promise. Now tip your head back so I can wash your hair. And I apologize in advance that your hair's gonna smell like," I reached down to the built-in bench and picked up my bottle of Old Spice shampoo, "Swagger."

"What's Swagger smell like?"

I tipped the bottle so she could look at it. After blinking several times, she gave up and loudly announced over the spray, "I can't read that with the torrential downpour and hurricane-like conditions."

"You don't like my hurricane?"

"I love it. Especially the two wall-mounted nozzles giving me a water massage. However, unless you have a pair of goggles handy, I'm afraid I cannot see the ingredient list. Not that I need to read them to know as long as it smells like you smell then I know it smells good."

Fuck, she was killing me.

I squirted a healthy glob of shampoo in my hand, set the shampoo down, and rubbed my hands together.

"Step outta the spray."

"Is that possible?"

"Step closer to me."

With my hands suspended above her shoulders, I waited for her to comply.

"I don't think that's a good idea."

"What?"

"You're naked."

Did she think I was going to attack her in the shower after she told me she was tired?

"And?"

"And, I'm naked. So I don't think that's a good idea."

"Baby, you're tired. I'm just gonna wash your hair."

Sloane slowly tipped her chin and leveled me with a look that had my cock jumping to attention.

"I could rally," she murmured.

My cock was wholly on board. Thankfully, at the moment, my brain seemed to be in charge.

"We'll see how you feel after I clean you up and get you into bed."

A ghost of a shadow moved over her face and I knew where her thoughts had turned. I'd turned her down twice and she thought I was doing it again, this time after I fucked her.

"I get it—"

If she'd planned on saying more she didn't get the chance before my hand shot out and I tagged her around the back of the neck. I pressed her body against mine right before my mouth went to hers. The moment our lips touched Sloane opened her mouth and my tongue swiped her bottom lip before finding hers and pushing it back into her mouth. With a fist full of hair, I tilted her head and took the kiss deeper. In response, Sloane's hands went to my ass. Her knee glided up my thigh and I hooked the back of it.

Then with a jump, her legs went around my waist. I twisted to the nozzle-free wall, pressed her back against it, and broke the kiss.

Well, fuck, that escalated quickly.

"I'm trying to take care of you."

I felt her shift. My hands gripped her ass tighter and I flexed my hips. I realized my mistake when I felt my shaft glide over her slick pussy, and she moaned when the head of my cock bumped her clit.

Fucking Christ.

"Sloane, baby, you're killing me."

"Why are you always saying that to me?"

"Because you push me to the brink of my control. Because when I'm with you self-preservation goes by the wayside. Because I'm confused as fuck and don't know what to do with you. I don't know how to make you stay. I don't want you to think I got you naked in the shower to fuck you. I wanted to take care of you. But like always, you look at me with those outrageously beautiful eyes and my thoughts turn. Because I don't want to fuck you in the shower. The next time I have you, I want you in bed. I don't want you tired and scared. I want your attention on me and what I'm doing to you. I want to learn every inch of you. I want to memorize the noises you make. I want to watch you come with my mouth between your legs and I want your mouth wrapped around my cock. But I can't say no to you and have you think I'm rejecting you."

I was concentrating so intently on deciphering the way Sloane was staring at me, I startled when her hands moved from my shoulders, up my neck, and then threaded into my wet hair. I was no closer to placing the expression when she softly asked, "You want me to stay?"

Time to man the fuck up.

"I want you to stay," I confirmed.

"For how long?"

For-fucking-ever.

"Long enough to give us a shot, to see if you like it."

I didn't need to study her expression to see her happiness. But all too soon it morphed into a frown.

"Elise. My apartment."

Fucking shit.

"We don't need to talk about this now," I told her.

"But you want me to stay?"

My heart clenched at the apprehension I heard.

"I want you to stay. But how about we finish our shower, get a good night's sleep, and table this discussion until you've had a few days to adjust."

"Okay."

I didn't hear any trepidation but still, I reiterated, "To be clear, and I know you can't miss this with my cock trying to tunnel his way past my control, but I want you. Right now though, I wanna take care of you a different way."

"I understand."

I stepped away from the wall and Sloane slid down the front of me but didn't step back when she landed on her feet. She wrapped her arms around me and pressed her cheek against my chest.

"Thank you for wanting to take care of me."

We stood in silence as I wondered what made Sloane so different that from across a crowded room I was instantly drawn to her. After a few moments of coming up blank, I wondered if I'd ever figure it out. Then I wondered if I cared that I'd never know. The answer to that was, I didn't care. She just felt right, and I was leaving it at that.

20

MY EYES SHOT open and I awoke with a start. There was banging. Lots and lots of loud banging.

It took me a second to remember I wasn't in California in my apartment. Which meant it took a second for me to remember the hard wall of muscle under my cheek wasn't my pillow. Memories of the night before started flashing—Asher's house, our shower, our near-sex in the shower, Asher washing me from top to toe making me feel cared for—no, he made me feel cherished. After that, he dried me off, toweled himself dry, gave me another one of his tees, then put me to bed. As soon as he came back from making sure the house was locked up, he curled me into him, and I was out.

Now my head was still resting on his chest. So was most of my upper body—one of my arms was over his stomach, the other trapped under me, and our legs were tangled.

Nice.

Beautiful.

I decided I wanted to wake up like this every morning for the rest of my life—minus the banging on the door.

"What's happening?" I croaked.

"Jesus," he groaned.

"Are you telling me our Lord and Savior is knocking on your door?" I mumbled.

I tilted my head back and caught sight of Asher's stubble. I was in deep thought about how those whiskers would feel grating on my thighs when I felt his body start to shake.

"No, baby, the Devil's knocking. Actually, my guess is there are two devils at the door. One of whom has a key."

"What?"

Before Asher could answer a woman's voice floated up the stairs.

"Rise and shine!"

Asher tightened his arm around me and he shoved his face in my neck. What he didn't do was get out of bed to see who was in his house shouting. Nor did he seem concerned.

"That's Letty," he told my throat.

"Maybe they're still sleeping. Rhode said they didn't get in until early this morning," a second woman said.

Asher kissed my neck, then dragged his lips up to my ear and informed me, "That's Brooklyn."

I attempted to keep the jealousy out of my tone when I asked, "Maybe you can explain who they are and why they have a key to your house."

Suddenly I was no longer pinning Asher to the bed. He rolled until he hovered over me. His face was still relaxed from sleep, and I decided I really wanted to see his face like that every morning, too.

"Cole told you about Letty. She's crazy, loud, and full of drama. Though she's not my woman so I find her drama hilarious. Seeing as her man, River, knew her for a decade before they got together and Letty is so full of drama there was no way she could've hidden it, he gets off on it and finds it funny, too. She's also loyal, kind, and a good friend to have. Brooklyn is down-to-earth and sweet. She balances Letty's crazy. She's not as loud but just as friendly. She and Rhode have a son, Remington. There's a long story there, one I'll tell you about it later when I'm not naked with a hard-on with my brothers' women in my living room."

And since he mentioned it, I became acutely aware he was naked, mostly on top of me, and his dick was indeed hard and pressing on my thigh.

"Why are they here?"

"Like I said, they're friendly."

"I was hoping to get friendly with you this morning."

Jeez, when had I become so forward?

Asher's face split into a smile. His head started to lower, his intent clear, but he halted his progress when Letty shouted again.

"It's one in the afternoon, Asher. Let her up for air, you beast! Sloane, knock twice if you need a rescue."

"Drama," Asher muttered.

"We're up!" he yelled back. "Give us a minute."

"You've had like seven million minutes. Hurry up."

"Jeez, Letty, leave them alone!" Brooklyn shouted. "Y'all take your time."

"Why are they here?" I repeated my question.

Asher brushed some of my hair off my face slowly while staring down at me and I knew he was thinking. I also knew when he'd figured out what he wanted to tell me when the creases around his eyes softened.

"They're here because they heard you were here, and they want to make sure you're okay. Rhode works with me, he talks to Brooklyn. Brooklyn talks to Letty. They don't know about Elise but they know I'm working undercover, they know you worked at the club. They know I brought you here because shit got hot in California. They're nosy, but it's not malice, it's concern. For you and for me."

"Why would they be concerned about me?"

"Baby, they know you're mine."

My chest started heaving as I struggled to expend the oxygen in my lungs. The depletion of air had nothing to do with Asher's heavy weight bearing down on me and everything to do with the emotions clogging my throat.

"How did this happen?"

"No clue. I just know it did. I fought it. I tried to leave you to your life in California. I tried not to be a selfish asshole, but I failed. And thinking on it, I always knew I wouldn't be able to walk away."

"If you don't hurry up, I'm coming up there and I don't care if I see your ding-a-ling."

Asher sighed and his eyes slowly drifted closed. He had an abundance of long lashes that matched his sandy brown hair. His brows were the same, brown mixed with some lighter shades. Though his stubble was darker, and I wondered if he grew a beard if it would be all brown or if some blond strands would appear. I took in his straight nose, square jaw, and full lips. He was total male perfection.

And mine.

How in the world had I gotten so lucky?

"You know," he started and opened his eyes, "this is one of those times I don't find Letty funny."

He didn't sound pleased about the interruption—actually, he sounded downright disgruntled.

"I think you need to put some clothes on," I grumbled.

Asher's lips turned down and his eyes got squinty.

"Are you pouting?" I asked.

"Men don't pout."

"It sure looks like you're pouting."

He ignored my assessment and dragged his hand from the side of my head down to cup my breast. He easily found my nipple and brushed his thumb back and forth over it until it pebbled.

"I had plans for you this morning," he reminded me. "Plans that included seeing how many orgasms I could wring out of you. So, I'm not pouting as much as I'm trying to find this shit funny instead of irritating."

"Ash?" Brooklyn called out from much closer than she was a few minutes ago.

Asher immediately yanked the covers over his bare ass and rolled until he was completely on top of me, shielding me from her view even though I was wearing a shirt.

"I'm just leaving clothes for Sloane," she rushed to say.

Then I heard footfalls on the steps. But I was only half paying attention to Brooklyn's retreat because when Asher rolled over me to protect my modesty, it put him between my legs, which meant his erection was dangerously close to where I wanted it. So close, all it would take was a thrust of his hips and he'd be inside of me.

"Don't fucking move," Asher ground out through gritted teeth.

I could feel Asher straining not to move. His face was a mask of pain and concentration. I did what I could to stay motionless but if he didn't get off me soon we were going to have a problem. Thankfully, Asher had more control than I did and he pushed himself to his knees.

This did nothing to help the state I was in. Asher gloriously naked—chest, abs, and hard dick on full display. My hands itched to touch him. My mouth watered. My pussy clenched.

"Christ, baby," he growled. "You keep looking at me like that, you're gonna be wearing my come."

I begrudgingly dragged my gaze from his erection, over his tightened abs, up to his face and was stunned at the ferocious appearance.

"Fuck," he snarled. "Tonight."

And with that, he rolled off me and off the bed. Last night I got my glimpse of him fully naked. Even tired, I still appreciated all that was Asher. But rested and completely awake in the daylight, I noticed the scratch marks from his shoulder blades to halfway down his back and I smiled.

It was crazy, possibly a little barbaric, but I couldn't deny I loved that he was wearing my marks. And knowing I gave him those while he was taking me, cementing our connection, I loved that more.

So when he came back fully dressed, he found me still in bed smiling.

"I'd ask you why you're smiling but I have a feeling whatever your answer is it's gonna make me want to fuck you so I'm not asking," he said on his way to the door.

I was positive if he knew what I was thinking he'd want to kick out the two Nosy Nellies downstairs and get back into bed with me.

He set a big plastic shopping bag down on the bed and rummaged through it, tossing a pair of panties in my direction. Next was a sports bra, then a pair of jeans, a t-shirt, and last a thick sweatshirt.

"Will these work?"

I snagged the undies and found the tag. Not my size but close enough.

"Yeah."

"I'll let you get dressed. I put out a new toothbrush for you. Floss and paste, left sink drawer. Today after we stop by the office we'll go shopping and get you everything you need."

"Okay."

"I'm going down to check on Letty and Brooklyn. With any luck, they've left, and we can bag on the office and spend the day in bed."

Even though he said it I knew he didn't mean it. There was obvious affection there and as nervous as I was, I was looking forward to meeting them.

"I'll be down in a minute." Asher was almost to the door when I asked, "By any chance do you have coffee?"

"Don't have a kitchen."

"Damn."

"There are literally fifteen coffee huts between here and the office. We'll stop."

"Okay, but I'm not responsible for my behavior until I get at least one cup in me."

From the doorway of his beautifully remodeled bedroom, Asher grinned. It wasn't a sexy smile, it wasn't huge, and it wasn't the kind that crinkled the corner of his eyes. It was a soft, sweet grin full of promise that made my stomach somersault.

"Noted."

———

WHAT A DIFFERENCE FIFTEEN MINUTES MAKES.

I was no longer looking forward to meeting Letty and Brooklyn. I was nervous as all get out, and with each step I took down the stairs, my nerves bunched tighter and tighter until I was two steps from the bottom and I came face-to-face with a raven-haired beauty. Then for some stupid reason, I panicked. Thankfully I didn't dart back up the stairs, but I did freeze. So did she as she took me in with a vacant look.

I struggled to find something to break the silence, no words coming to me as the woman continued to stare. Then she smiled, which made her even more beautiful.

"Good, they fit!" she happily exclaimed. "Cole's idea of help was to tell me you had a rocking body with great legs and big boobs. After a ten-minute conversation where he rattled off ten celebrities he thought you looked like, I realized talking to him was a waste of time. So I had to guess. I'm Letty by the way."

I took a breath but before I could introduce myself she went on.

"Not that Cole wasn't right, you totally have great legs, do you run? And I didn't know what Cole's definition of big boobs was and honestly, love the man like a brother but the topic of boobs wasn't something I wanted to discuss so you're stuck with a sports bra until we can get to the mall. Asher said you needed coffee so we'll do that first, then hit Macy's. After that, we'll hang at my bookstore while Asher works."

"Um..."

Asher had said there were fifteen coffee huts nearby and I wondered if Letty had hit them all on her way over.

"Zip it, Letty, you're scaring her."

Yes, Letty was scaring the pants off me.

I took in the other woman, who was obviously Brooklyn. She, too, was beautiful. Long brown hair with artfully placed blond streaks. If I was staying in Idaho, I was definitely asking her for the name of the salon she went to.

"Hi. I'm Brooklyn."

"Nice to meet you, I'm Sloane." I looked back at Letty, feeling the need to say something to her. "Nice to meet you, too, Letty. And thank you for braving a conversation with

Cole about my sizes." Then I asked her what I really wanted to know. "You own a bookstore?"

She gave me a megawatt smile and nodded. "Do you like to read?"

"Yes. But I mostly read romance."

"Girlll," she drawled. "You are in luck. My store is romance only. Every genre you can think of. What are you reading right now?"

My nerves started to recede. I could talk about books all day long.

"The last few months have been crazy so I've barely had time to read. But I did download the new Caitlyn O'Leary book the other day."

"No shit!" Letty clapped and her gaze went to Brooklyn. "See? Totally meant to be."

The back door opened and Asher stepped into the house with a smile. I took in his beanie-covered head and snow-covered boots and almost laughed. What a stark difference from the mild winter we were having back in California. The beaches were no longer filled with tourists but the locals who were used to the frigid Pacific were still surfing.

"Yep. Meant to be," Brooklyn agreed.

"What's meant to be?" Asher asked.

How in the heck had I missed the huge wall of windows? Last night, sure, it was dark outside and there was only one standing lamp illuminating the space. But now, light streamed through them, revealing a huge deck that looked like it was freshly shoveled which would explain what Asher was doing outside. Beyond that stretched a wooded area, and off in the distance I could see the top of a huge snow-covered mountain.

It was a winter wonderland.

Holy shit, Asher had the most beautiful view I'd ever seen.

"You and Sloane." Letty's answer snapped my attention back to her. "She's reading Caitlyn O'Leary's new release, *Her Unflinching Hero*."

Asher's hands came up and covered his ears before he proclaimed, "No spoilers! I haven't started."

So, my jaw might've hit the unfinished, dirty wood planks. My eyes might've also widened five times their normal size. And I was pretty sure I was sputtering when I blurted, "What?"

"Oh, Asher didn't tell you he belongs to a book club?" Letty grinned. "All the guys do."

"You read Caitlyn O'Leary?" I asked Asher.

"Do I read Caitlyn O'Leary?" he scoffed. "I finished the Night Storm books and went straight to Omega Sky, and I never miss a livestream with her and John."

"John?"

"Oh, girl." Asher laughed. "You can't call yourself a fan if you don't know John."

I glanced at Brooklyn who was shaking her head in amusement.

"Don't listen to him. He had no idea who John was until he came to Smutties one day when me and Letty were watching one of their lives and John was doing a read-thru of one of Caitlyn's books. John is Caitlyn's husband. He's hilarious and gives Caitlyn shit nonstop."

"Smutties?"

"That's the name of my bookstore," Letty proudly told me. "Only smut books on my shelves."

"Oh my God, I can't wait to see it."

"Then grab your purse and let's roll," Brooklyn invited.

Without warning a memory of the day I met Elise filled

my mind. She was my waitress and since I was eating alone, I was reading a book and as it turned out she was reading the same one. We instantly hit it off. I stayed at my table well after I'd finished eating and between checking on her tables, she stood beside mine and chatted with me. When it was time for me to leave we exchanged numbers. From that day on, we talked every day. That was, until the morning I woke up and realized she never made it home from the club.

"Sloane?" I jolted when Asher's arms went around my waist and I tipped my head back to find his gentle eyes full of concern. "You okay?"

"Yeah. I was just thinking."

"Baby," he whispered.

I might've been in Idaho because being in California was too dangerous, but I couldn't help thinking I was exactly where I was supposed to be at exactly the time I was supposed to be there.

"I'm fine. Are you coming with us or going to the office?"

"Do you want me to come with you?"

I thought about how friendly Letty and Brooklyn were and how long it had been since I'd had girl time. Time to gossip and laugh and drink coffee or wine and eat crap food full of carbs and laugh some more. I thought about how much I missed Elise and how much she would love Letty and Brooklyn.

So really, there wasn't much to think about.

"You go to the office."

"You sure?"

"Yep."

Asher studied me a beat before he bent down and gave me a lip brush.

"I'm giving you cash, use it for everything. Clothes,

coffee, books, whatever you buy. Absolutely no credit cards and no ATM machines."

I wanted to argue about Asher giving me money, but I knew he was right. I could be tracked if I used my bank card.

"Okay. I don't need much, and I'll pay you back."

"Sure."

Something told me his quick acquiescence was a lie, but before I could call him on it Letty started bossing.

"Alright, lovebirds, break apart." Letty clapped her hands and started for the front door. "Sadie's already texted twice asking when she gets to meet you, so we have to hurry."

"Sloane'll be right out," Asher said.

"Jacket and boots," Brooklyn blurted. "Boots are by the door. I hope they fit. I brought you a jacket, but I forgot it in the car. We'll go out to get it and give you two some... um...privacy."

Brooklyn moved over to her friend and tugged her elbow when she didn't move.

"C'mon," Brooklyn urged.

"Fine. But if they start making out and Sadie texts again, you're gonna talk to her."

The two women walked out the door and my attention went back to Asher.

"They're good people and they'll take care of you. Sadie is my teammate Reese's wife. She owns the bakery next door to Smutties. She's a little shy at first but it doesn't take her long to warm up."

"I'll be fine."

"If you need me, call me or have one of the girls call me. When I'm at the office I'll grab you a burner phone."

"Oh, I've never had a burner," I teased. "Now I'm like a real-life fugitive."

As intended, Asher chuckled but his amusement didn't last long.

"Fair warning, I'm gonna make it so you never want to leave."

He wouldn't have to work that hard to make me stay, though I didn't get a chance to tell him that because his mouth was on mine.

And just as Letty had predicted, Asher and I made out in his wreck of a living room. A beautiful open space that when finished would be spectacular.

And as I kissed him, I hoped with everything inside of me I got to help him complete it.

21

"AND THAT'S EVERYTHING."

I was sitting in the back corner of Smutties in one of Letty's kickass purple velvet chairs. Sadie was sitting in the matching chair to my right and Brooklyn and Letty were on a two-seater couch. I'd just finished telling them the story of Elise.

Earlier, Brooklyn and Letty had taken me to get coffee and I learned what a coffee hut was. Further, I learned that Idaho coffee brewed in what looked like a tiny house on the side of the road was better than any coffee I'd had in California. I wasn't sure if it was the chilly air, the snow-covered mountains all around me, the friendly service, or the company. But it was excellent. I'd scratched good coffee onto the Reasons To Stay In Idaho list.

After coffee pick-up, we went to Macy's and grabbed a few things. But then the girls took me to North 40 Outfitters where Brooklyn kitted me out in winter gear and boots. According to Letty, temperatures had been mild but they were expecting a cold snap. Seeing as the last time it snowed in The Valley was sometime in the Sixties and in

SoCal fifty degrees was considered freezing, I didn't particularly agree with Letty's definition of mild.

Once the girls were satisfied I wasn't going to freeze to death during my stay, we headed to Treats. As soon as we walked into the cute bakery and I took in the pastel-pink accents and dark gray walls along with the black and white chevron tiles, I fell in love. I *immediately* scribbled Treats onto the Reasons To Stay In Idaho list under amazing coffee. And that was before I'd met Sadie and tried her lemon poppyseed muffins. After my second muffin, I'd moved Treats up to the number one spot.

Asher had been right, Sadie was shy. But he was also right when he said she warmed up quickly. It might've been her watching me with a smile as I shoved the last of my second muffin in my mouth and declared around a mouthful that she was a culinary goddess. Or maybe it was the way Letty and Brooklyn had easily accepted me. Either way, Sadie was open and friendly and had the prettiest blue eyes I'd ever seen.

Our visit was cut short when Letty got a call saying she was needed at the bookstore. I was dying to browse her shelves and Sadie shooed us off with the promise she'd be over shortly. It was then I met Mrs. Simpson. The very second I spotted the old woman I knew I wanted to grow up to be her. She was the spitting image of Liz Taylor—old, glamorous Hollywood with a perfectly styled short hairdo, a face full of makeup, dressed to the nines, along with tasteful but elegant jewelry. She looked ready to walk the red carpet, not work the checkout counter of a bookstore in Coeur d'Alene. After a quick but formal introduction— because of course Mrs. Simpson would be proper and reserved—Brooklyn whisked me away to show me around.

During my tour, I learned that Brooklyn was a voice

actor and narrated audiobooks. She also had a booth in the back of Smutties where she worked. It was a tossup, and I was torn between all the beautiful love stories in paperback form and going into the back to watch Brooklyn work. The books won out but only because Brooklyn had taken the day off and she'd offered to let me come back anytime to watch.

Anytime.

That was what she'd said.

The same as Sadie had told me to come back to Treats, *anytime.*

The same as Letty had offered to take me to Spokane to shop, *anytime.*

Now was now, and I'd spilled my guts, leaving all three women staring at me with what looked like extreme anger mixed with compassion.

"And just like that, you believed Asher when he told you he was undercover?" Brooklyn asked.

I shrugged not knowing how to explain why exactly I'd believed him.

"I guess I just knew there was something off. He'd spent months in the club and hadn't touched a single woman. Who pays all that money to belong to a sex club and then not have sex? And he looked seriously dejected every time he walked into a viewing room. Call it intuition or instinct but I trusted him."

"Would you call it love?" Brooklyn pushed.

"I fell in love with him before I knew his name was Asher."

"That's so sweet," Sadie put in.

I didn't know if it was sweet or crazy.

"Wait." Letty leaned forward and said, "Let's go back to the part where your friends stopped calling."

"I was brushing them off. Every waking moment I spent

trying to find Elise or coming up with ways to find Elise or on the phone with the police. I didn't have time for them, so they quit calling."

I had no idea why I was defending my old friends. If I had to guess, I'd say it was habit or some sense of loyalty even though they'd easily turned their backs on me. Something that cut deep.

"Um, no!" Brooklyn snapped. "Just no. They were Elise's friends, too. Their every waking moment should've been trying to find Elise. And if they couldn't do that, then they should've spent their every waking moment supporting you."

As soon as Brooklyn finished, Sadie jumped in. "Brook's right. It's not like you got a boyfriend and ditched them. Though at the beginning of a new relationship a friend knows things are intense and gives you space to spend time with your man. But you weren't *brushing* them off, you were being a friend. Not just a good friend—a true friend."

Hold it together, Sloane.

My gaze found the floor. I knew they were right; I hadn't blown off my friends or ditched them or brushed them off. They'd let me down, but worse—they let down Elise. So even if I could've forgiven them for turning on me I would never forgive them for giving up on Elise.

"So what now?" Letty asked.

I lifted my eyes and asked, "What now?"

"What's next? What do we do to help? You said the guys are working on it and that's huge, they're good at what they do—the best, actually. But while they're looking into it what do we do?"

I sat there in stunned silence.

Not, what *can* we do to help?

What *do* we do?

Do.

I'd met these women hours ago and they were no-questions-asked on board to help me find Elise.

I looked between the three of them and I knew down to my bones if one of them went missing the other two would stop at nothing to get her back. They'd give up their lives. They'd quit their jobs. They'd work in a sex club to try to find answers. They'd do anything.

Letty, Brooklyn, and Sadie weren't friends—they were sisters not of the heart but of the soul. They were the truest kind of friends.

They were who I needed six months ago.

"I don't know. Yesterday everything happened so quickly, then we came here, and I haven't had a chance to talk to Asher about what they're doing."

"No, Sloane." Letty shook her head. "The guys have taken over looking for Elise. You let them do what they're trained to do and you keep yourself safe. What I'm asking is, what do you need? What do we do to help you?"

Help *me*?

My gaze hit the floor again—this time to hide the tears that formed. But it was no use, I couldn't hide my shoulders shaking and I couldn't hide the sob that tore from my chest. Sadie reached over, grabbed my hand, and just held on. She didn't squeeze. She didn't tug it to get my attention. She simply held on.

Just like Elise would've done.

Just like Elise had done over the years.

"I don't understand," I said through a hiccupped cry.

"What don't you understand?" Sadie asked softly.

"How do you turn your back on someone you love?"

"You don't, Sloane." Sadie's voice was no longer sweet, it was full of vigor and anger, and that was when I felt it—

the piercing pain of Sadie's words puncturing my heart. "You *never* turn your back on the people you love." I felt those words thread through my heart. "Never. You never leave a friend to go at it alone. Whatever the *it* is they need you to stand by them. Those women were not your friends, they weren't Elise's, and you're better off without them."

And when Sadie was done the first stitch was complete. The first step, the first suture of many that I needed to close the big, gaping hole in my heart.

"Thank you."

"I know she didn't just say thank you," Letty muttered. "You do not thank your girls for listening. You do not thank your girls when you're carrying a heavy burden and they lend an ear. That's what being a friend *is*. You thank a friend when they tell you about a kickass shoe sale. You thank a friend when they recommend a good book. You do not thank a friend for being a friend. Would you thank Elise for listening to you after you had a hard day?"

Shot. To. The. Heart.

Another stitch.

"Yes, I would thank her, and she'd roll her eyes, tell me to shut up, and toss the remote at me and tell me it was my turn to pick the TV show we were going to watch even if it was her turn. And if I had a particularly bad day she'd even let me watch a cooking show even though she knew I had no intentions of learning how to cook."

"That's a damn good friend right there," Brooklyn mumbled, then looked at Letty. "Don't get any ideas. You know I love you, but you'd have to lose a toe or be in a full body cast before I watched a cooking show with you."

Letty ignored Brooklyn and moved the conversation to a new topic.

"Now that we've come to an agreement your fake friends were bitches, I have more questions."

"Oh, boy," Sadie grumbled and squeezed my hand. "Brace, girl, I know that look."

Another stitch.

Apparently, Letty didn't need my encouragement to ask what was on her mind and she took no offense at Sadie's comment because she launched right in.

"So, you met Asher while you were both working undercover at a sex club, and you thought his name was Adam?"

After Sadie's dire warning I wasn't expecting Letty to lob such an innocuous question my way.

"Yeah."

"And in this sex club, there were people having sex?"

Funny how twenty-four hours ago I didn't want to talk about the club but now it didn't bother me. I wasn't sure if it was because I knew I'd never work there again or if I felt comfortable with the girls, or if instinctively I knew they wouldn't judge me. But whatever the reason, I was no longer embarrassed. Actually, I was proud of my tenure as the event coordinator at Club Joi. Proud because I was the kind of friend worthy of Elise, worthy of Letty, Brooklyn, and Sadie.

"Yes, Letty. There were lots of people having sex and watching sex and inviting people to watch and join."

"Wow. I've never been to a sex club," Brooklyn informed me.

"In my opinion, you're not missing much. Unless that's your kink, then you should go."

"Oh my God!" Letty chortled. "Can you imagine the look on Dulles's face if you told him you wanted to go to a sex club?"

"Yes, Lets, I can imagine," Brooklyn returned. "It's the same face River would give you."

Dulles?

"Wait, who's Dulles?"

"Letty's nickname for Rhode," Sadie filled me in. "It's a long story but Rhode and Brooklyn had a hot, steamy one-night stand. Brooklyn was channeling a sassy book heroine and decided not to exchange names with Rhode. Which proved to be a huge error when a few months later she wound up pregnant. Since Brooklyn didn't know Rhode's name and the baby-making happened at a hotel in D.C. next to the airport, Letty called him Dulles. And now she calls him that just to annoy him."

Um. Wait. What?

I transferred my stare to Brooklyn to check her reaction to Sadie spilling her very private business. Not that I thought Sadie would speak out of turn maliciously but I just met these women.

"True story. That's what happened," Brooklyn said. "And I didn't find him until he was working a case in Spokane which involved Letty's sister."

I glanced at Letty, and she picked up the conversation.

"My sister and I weren't close, but she was my sister and I loved her. In her life, she did some pretty horrible things to me and to Brooklyn. Kiki's death was tragic, but her sacrifice was not."

All those stitches were threatening to tear back open at the sadness in Letty's tone.

"I'm sorry you lost her, but I'm especially sorry you weren't close while she was alive."

"I've made peace with it." Letty held my eyes. There was lingering grief but there was something else shining—understanding, maybe compassion, hope.

The bell chimed, breaking the moment. Letty's gaze broke away from mine and she looked over my shoulder.

"Well, damn it all to hell. The guys are here and we didn't even get to the good stuff."

Sadie slipped her hand from mine, turned in her chair, and the look on her face told me her husband had entered the store.

"You mean, you didn't get to ask Sloane if she and Asher got busy at the club?" Brooklyn rushed out.

"Like you don't want to know?" Letty shot back.

"We didn't...or we kinda did, but not like that."

Brooklyn's eyes widened comically as she scooted to the edge of the couch. "What does that mean?"

"Why does it look like the four of you are up to no good?" a deep, masculine voice said from behind me.

"You're interrupting," Letty complained.

"Hey, baby." I heard then a moment later I felt Asher's lips on my head.

I tipped my head back and stared up at Asher's upside-down smiling face.

"Hey."

"Good day?"

One of the best.

"Yes."

His smile got bigger, and I felt another stitch pull tight.

"Good. Ready to go to dinner?"

I righted my head and turned in my chair, noticing it was dark outside.

Holy crap, where had the day gone?

Coffee, shopping, and girl time. That was where it went, and what better way than to spend the day?

Once the shock of losing track of time wore off, I was shocked in an entirely different way. Standing next to Asher and Cole were two very handsome men. My eyes darted between them in an attempt to ascertain if I was seeing things. They were all similar in height and build. One had darker hair than the rest and one had crazy cool greenish brown eyes.

And it was the one with the cool eyes who broke the silence. "I heard you ate the last two muffins."

That was also the deep voice I'd heard when the guys came in.

"Um...what?"

"My lemon poppyseed muffins."

Was he saying I ate his muffins?

"I ate your muffins?"

"Yep."

"Reese, not every lemon poppyseed muffin is yours," Sadie thankfully cut in. "Sloane, this is my husband, Reese. He's a little crazy about my muffins."

Cole's face split into a huge smile that could be described as naughty.

"Yeah, Reese, we all know how much you love her *muffins*."

My eyes were bouncing back and forth between Reese and Cole when the other man introduced himself.

"I'm Rhode. Nice to meet you."

So this was Dulles. I could totally see why Brooklyn would be up for a no-names-one-night-stand.

"Nice to meet you. I'm Sloane."

Rhode's lips twisted into a smirk and I was damn happy I was still sitting.

"Don't worry, girl," Letty started. "We were the same way when they rolled into town. But trust me, their looks wear off. And you're left with a group of men who behave like boys."

"Tell me about it," I griped. "You tell one story about busting a nut and they take it and run straight to the gutter."

The room erupted into laughter, and as the volume rose, I felt the piercing pain of more stitches. I felt a warmth come over me that reminded me just how cold I'd been.

"Is there another way to bust a nut? I—"

Before Rhode could finish his sentence, Cole stepped in. "I wouldn't ask that. Asher gets touchy about his woman talking about nut-busting."

"Maybe we should stop talking about this," Asher suggested.

"Why? You're the one who taught me how to bust a nut," I countered. "If you like talking about nuts busting you should've called it something different, like scrotum smashing or testicle traumatization."

"I like her," Reese announced. "I've decided to share my muff—"

"No one's sharing a damn thing with my woman."

At Asher's outburst, I looked back at the girls. "Asher doesn't like to share. As in, ever, not at all. But in this case, he's gonna have to learn because those muffins are at the top of my Reasons To Stay In Idaho list."

"Seriously?" Asher groaned. "A muffin is above me?"

"My woman makes damn good muffins, brother."

After everyone settled down from a second round of laughter, Asher pulled me up from my chair and told me to say goodbye. Which I did, coupled with hugs for the girls and a promise I'd text everyone later with my temporary number. Asher damn near dragged me out of the bookstore, ignoring his friends' comments about him being in a hurry. Truth be told, I was in a hurry, too. As much as I'd needed some girl time, I wanted time with Asher alone. No sex club. No Cole and Wilson. No Lorenzo. No investigation.

Just us.

The cold air smacked me in the face just as Asher spun me around to face him.

"Muffins are above me?" he growled.

"Well, so far you've made some pretty lofty promises you've yet to make good on, so, yes," I teased.

"I washed your hair and gave you a scalp massage."

"You did."

"And I washed you."

He had washed me. From my neck to my feet, he'd lathered me up and it was heavenly.

"That was last night," I reminded him. "And last night you were at the top of my list. Today I had Sadie's muffins, after I had really great coffee. By the way, that's on the list, too. So are Brooklyn, Sadie, Letty, and Mrs. Simpson."

"Am I even on the list?"

At the seriousness of his question, I slid my hands up his biceps, over his shoulders, and laced my fingers behind his neck.

"I was teasing," I whispered. And just to punctuate my sincerity, I rolled up on my toes and gave him a peck on the corner of his mouth.

Asher didn't much feel like accepting my peck. I knew because before I could pull my mouth from his, he turned his head and captured my lips. He further demonstrated this by taking my kiss from street legal straight to deep, wet, and lewd.

After he was done kissing me stupidly, he pulled back— but not far—to ask, "Wanna know what's on the top of my list?"

"What list?" I was positive I sounded as breathless as I felt, and I didn't give two finger-licking fucks.

"It doesn't have a name," he told me.

"You have a list without a name?"

I watched up close as Asher smiled and couldn't help but return his grin.

"I just made it up."

"Does this list include things like, say, feeding me dinner?"

"Sure, it's a broad and all-encompassing list. Though feeding you dinner isn't number one."

The chill in the air made me shiver but I didn't mind this kind of cold. The kind that meant I was outside on a beautiful winter night with a handsome man bantering on the street after he kissed me breathless. I'd take this kind of cold any day of the week.

"Okay, I'll bite, what's number one?"

"The way you light up when you're happy. Your sense of humor. How you kiss. How loyal you are. How deeply you love. Your trust. And the fact you'd make a list of reasons to stay in Idaho and Brooklyn, Letty, and Sadie are on that list."

Another stitch, this one the most painful of them all.

But since I'd already had two breakdowns in front of him and I felt another one threatening, I opted to tuck away his words and keep them for later.

"And Mrs. Simpson. I've decided when I'm her age I'm gonna be just like her."

"She's a wise woman."

"I'm not talking about her wisdom, Asher. I mean when I am her age, I'm going full-blown old Hollywood throwback, and that will include wearing three strands of pearls while working in a bookstore."

"Won't be hard for you to accomplish, seeing as you're already a bombshell."

"You do know you're at the top of my list, right?"

Asher studied me a beat before he dropped his head to mine.

"I do now."

Something else struck me as we were standing on the sidewalk in front of Smutties.

Asher was easy.

Easy to talk to.

Easy to be around.

Easy to be honest with.

I didn't have to guard my thoughts or feelings. I didn't have to wonder if I was sharing too much or going too fast or too slow. Asher was right there next to me keeping in step. He was open and honest and was quick to share his thoughts and feelings.

Just *easy*.

———

"*ASHER*."

His name came out as two breathy syllables. Not taking his mouth off my pussy he growled. My hips came off the bed as my climax shot through me.

Glorious.

My orgasm was still pulsing when Asher came up on his knees, draped my legs over his thighs, and thrusted deep. Every millimeter of my skin buzzed. Asher was watching me watch him as he took me rough.

"Hands above your head, baby."

I lifted my hands above my head, felt the headboard, and needed no further instruction. As soon as my palms were flat against the wood, he powered forward. My body jolted with every hard drive. One of his hands went to my hip and the other went between my legs. His thumb hit just the right spot and the impossible happened. As one orgasm slipped away a second built.

The pleasure was so intense my eyelids grew heavy. My breathing turned shallow. Asher's was labored. Grunts, groans, and panting filled the room. I didn't know who was making which sound, just that I loved it as they mingled together. I was close and getting closer.

So good.

The best.

The very, *very* best.

"So goddamned gorgeous taking my cock."

"So goddamned gorgeous giving it to me," I panted my response.

Asher drilled deep. His controlled thrusts turned desperate. I pushed back on the headboard the best I could until my orgasm exploded, tearing me open and leaving me crying out his name. I knew he was joining me when his fingers dug into my hips, and he slammed his dick to the root and groaned my name.

Since I no longer needed my hands to keep me stationary, I lifted them and then realized I couldn't reach Asher.

"Come closer."

Keeping us connected, he dropped forward. My arms went around his shoulders, my head came off the pillow, and I kissed him.

He allowed this for approximately six seconds before he took over. I didn't mind—he was a good kisser.

It was sometime later after I'd cleaned up and gotten back into bed. After I found that the two other times I'd slept next to Asher and he cuddled me all night weren't a fluke. He wanted me close and had no problem telling me verbally and nonverbally. So, like last night, my head was on his chest, our legs were tangled together, and my arm was resting slanted across his stomach.

"Thank you for going to dinner with me."

I blinked into the darkness.

I did this rapidly to hold my emotions at bay.

Dinner had been great. Asher had asked about my day and filled me in on the Rhode, Brooklyn, Remington story, which was both tragic and beautiful since they ended up together as a family. But in telling me about the trio's reunion he also told me about Letty's sister and how she died. He didn't let me dwell on her murder, taking us right into Letty and River and how they'd known each other for over a decade but only met face-to-face recently and now they were engaged. He asked about shopping. We talked books. I teased him about reading romance, then told him I loved that he did.

It was easy.

Then we came home, and he set about making good on his earlier promises. Which of course he did, spectacularly.

"I think I'm supposed to thank you," I whispered.

"Why would you thank me? I'm the one who had the pleasure of your company."

The blinking continued when I begged, "Please stop talking. I'm afraid you'll run if I cry three days in a row."

"Okay, I'll stop."

Which thankfully he did. I was nearly asleep when I heard him whisper.

"I will never run from you."

My eyes popped open. My breath caught and I prayed he was telling the truth.

I wasn't ruined.

I was on the mend.

22

I WAS at my desk reading the latest intel report on Will Evans. He was in frequent contact with all the usual suspects—Russian mob, cartels, and warlords—but none of those interested me. Getting a Russian mobster to roll over was akin to making wine out of water, and since I wasn't Jesus I'd never pull off that particular miracle. It was the *Lorenzos* he dealt with, the middlemen, we needed to find. I had less than a week before I had to be back in California. Something I was hoping to avoid.

I heard footsteps outside my office and looked up from the papers scattered on my desk.

"You got a minute?" Wilson asked.

I didn't like the look on my boss's face. Normally, Wilson was easygoing. That was until you pissed him off—then the man was like a Rottie on steroids. He'd chew your leg off and not think twice.

"What are you doing here?"

"The team's waiting in the conference room."

What the fuck? Wilson had called a meeting and no one told me.

"The team's waiting?"

Wilson held my angry stare. And since I knew he wasn't going to break I pushed back from the desk and stood.

A hundred scenarios played out in my mind as I followed Wilson down the hall. Yesterday he'd finally met with Marco Kelly, the owner of Club Joi. I knew the meeting happened, but after a brief check-in Wilson said he had some business to handle, then he went dark. However, he had not mentioned coming back to Idaho.

As soon as I walked into the room all eyes came to me.

Seriously, what the fuck?

Thankfully, Wilson didn't make me wait.

"To say Marco Kelly is pissed that his son is involved in trafficking would be an understatement. To say he's fucking furious his son brought it to his beloved club would be a serious fucking understatement. Of those two things, I reckon Marco's more pissed that his squeaky-clean club has been under investigation and why. Marco has secondary security systems in all his clubs. Only he and his lawyer have access to them. During our meeting, he called his lawyer and asked him to review the footage of the day the guy on horseback saw the girl running naked on the property." Wilson paused and inhaled deeply. "Her name was Michelle Kendrick. She was found dead in Palmdale two days after she was at the mansion."

"Fuck!" I yanked out an empty chair between Jack and Cole and sat.

"There was some back and forth between Marco and his lawyer. But as I said, Marco's more worried about his clubs than he is about his son. Part of this is because Lorenzo's been a pain in Marco's ass for years. Lorenzo's supposed to be in California on a time-out from running Marco's other business ventures into the ground. In an effort to save

Club Joi's reputation and keep the police from further investigating the club, he agreed to help. All of the mansion's security footage has been turned over to the Marshal Service."

Fucking, fucking hell.

"Inside and out?" I tightly inquired.

I didn't need to ask more than that. Wilson knew what I was asking.

"Common areas only and last night Shep got into Lorenzo's computer and downloaded all the footage from the cameras he set up and wiped his machine. For the time being, I've asked Shep to hold on to the footage in case we need it but I didn't turn it over to the Marshals."

"Where's Lorenzo?" Rhode asked.

"Incarcerated."

"What about Will Evans?"

Wilson's angry gaze swung my way, and I knew I wasn't going to like his answer.

"In the wind. So far, nothing puts him at the club while Michelle was there."

Fucking shit. We'd lost that lead.

"Something else," Wilson started but stopped and stared at Cole for a moment before he came back to me and closed his eyes.

Fuck.

"He knows Sloane overheard his conversation," I guessed and stood.

I had to get to Sloane and get her someplace where neither of us could be traced.

Fucking shit.

Cole followed me up and his hand went to my shoulder. I shrugged it off but Cole stepped in front of me.

"Move."

"I will," he said. "We will. We move as a team, and we don't have all the intel. Calm down and wait."

"It's not Will, Asher," Wilson announced. I felt my chest loosen right before Wilson dropped the bomb. "I'm sorry, brother, there's no easy way to tell you this. Elise's body has been found."

Jesus fuck.

Sloane was going to be devastated. Straight up, to her core shattered.

"Where?" I clipped.

"Florida. Shep never had any luck running the plates of the members who were at the club the night she went missing because she was taken by helicopter. Marco's cameras caught the tail number. Shep ran it and found the owner. I called in a favor and the FBI sent agents out. Her body was found buried in his backyard."

"How long has she been dead?"

I wasn't sure what the right answer was. Any amount of time meant she was still gone. But if it was recent, Sloane would blame herself.

"Long enough the body decomp was so bad they had to use dental records. They found two other bodies. One was bones, the other was fresh."

"Jesus," Cole spat.

"The FBI has notified Elise's parents. I've also been in contact with them, explained the situation, and I asked them to let us tell Sloane. They agreed to wait for her call."

Thank fuck Wilson had the foresight to contact the Kellers and ask them to hold off calling her.

"Appreciate that."

"You know we all have her back," Wilson proclaimed.

I glanced around the room and each of my teammates wore similar expressions. Even Jack and Davis who had never met her, but they'd have her back because she was mine. I'd never regretted or second-guessed leaving the FBI. But right then, seeing my teammates ready and waiting to pitch in and do what they could to lessen the unbearable pain Sloane was getting ready to endure only reinforced that I'd made the right decision.

"Appreciate that, too. I want to tell her alone. But I need Brooklyn, Sadie, and Letty on call."

"Done," Rhode and Reese said in unison.

"Before I go, is there anything else I need to know?"

"Our part in California is done now that Marco's cooperating. Otis Craven was arrested last night. The FBI's working him now. Hopefully, he flips soon. Will Evans is known to every three-letter agency, but no one's ever been able to pin anything on him. Otis and Lorenzo are fucked—hopefully, one of them will turn on Evans."

Otis Craven.

Fitting name for a filthy, spineless motherfucker.

May he rot in hell.

"I'll have my phone—"

"Off," Wilson incorrectly finished my sentence. "Keep your phone off and take care of your woman. We'll handle everything else."

I let the gratitude I felt wash over me.

Then I left to break my woman's heart.

———

"ARE you gonna teach me how to putty?" Sloane asked.

I never knew there was a cowardly side to me. But looking at Sloane's bright, happy face waving a putty knife at the wall in my living room, I almost said yes. There were approximately seven hundred nail holes that needed to be patched. I could spend the rest of the afternoon listening to her tell me all about watching Brooklyn narrate while we worked side by side. When we finished puttying, I could teach her how to sand the floor. Hell, I could put off telling her about Elise for at least six months.

Fuck, I was a pussy.

And an asshole.

Sloane needed to know.

I just wasn't ready to see her brightness dim. I wasn't ready for her to turn me away.

Fucking hell, how selfish was I?

"Baby, I need to talk to you about something."

Smooth, asshole.

"Everything okay?"

No, I'm about to blow your world up.

I made my way to her, pulled the putty knife out of her hand, and tossed it on the banged-up floor, uncaring if there was another nick in the wood.

"Put your arms around me."

"Asher?"

"Please, baby, trust me. Put your arms around me."

She did as I asked. I lifted my hands and cupped her jaw, gently holding her hostage.

It took two tries to swallow the lump in my throat. Two tries before I got the words out.

"The FBI found Elise. I'm so sorry..."

I got no more out before Sloane's blood-curdling scream filled the room. I quickly shifted and scooped her up into my arms. Her sobs started before I hit the first step and only got louder and louder the closer I got to my bedroom. I put a knee on the mattress and twisted around to my ass, keeping Sloane cradled as I sat with my back to the headboard.

"I'm sorry, baby. So fucking sorry."

She shoved her face into my neck and continued to cry. I rested my cheek on the top of her head and held on.

Never in my life had I felt so useless. There was nothing I could do for her to make this better. There were no words to erase her pain. All I could do was hold on to her while she shook in my arms with big body-wracking, uncontrollable tears.

"I got you, Sloane. Anything you need, baby, I got you."

Her body bucked followed by a pain-filled shriek.

"Hold on to me, Sloane."

She pressed closer.

I wrapped my arms tighter.

This went on for a long time. Slowly, her sobs turned into crying, then the crying became intermittent. Until she went completely quiet.

"Sloane?"

"I knew," she whispered. "I think I always knew but my heart refused to let me believe it. I needed to have hope. Until she was found, I had to hold on to a sliver of hope, so that if a miracle happened, she'd know I never stopped believing. But she doesn't get a miracle."

Christ.

The timing was fucked, totally jacked, but I finally understood Sloane's draw. I loved the way she loved. I loved the loyalty. I loved her bravery. But it was more than that. Sloane's draw was her hope—she was blinded by it. Against all odds, she remained faithful to it—steadfast in her determination not to let it go.

We settled in the silence until Sloane fell asleep.

I tipped my head back and stared at my ceiling as I held my woman while she slept.

I did this hoping Sloane would allow me to see her through the days to come.

23

I WOKE up this morning cradled in Asher's arms.

He'd spent the whole night sitting.

He never let me go. Even when I woke up and tried to sneak away to wash my face and brush my teeth. The moment I moved, his arms became steel bands and locked me in place.

On the worst night of my life, Asher had me.

The morning after learning my best friend had been murdered, Asher had me.

It was strange how something horrible and tragic and devastatingly heartbreaking can open your eyes. Waking up surrounded by Asher, I finally understood. I didn't see him across the room and fall in love with him. *I felt him.* I felt his comfort. I felt his protection. I felt him in a visceral way.

That might sound crazy but that was the truth.

"I need to get up," I told him.

"In a minute."

I knew he wanted to know how I was doing but I also knew he wouldn't ask because who wants to ask someone who lost someone important to them how they were doing?

The obvious answer was, not well. The honest answer was, life fucking sucks right now.

"I'm angry," I told him the truth. "I'm really angry I'll never see her again. I'm mad I'll never hear her voice again. I feel hateful and full of rage. I'm confused. I have so many questions, but I know I'm not ready for you to tell me what happened and where she was found. I'm not sure if I ever want to know and that's not me being in denial. It's me preserving her life. She is not how she died, and I don't ever want to think of her like that. Elise was sweet and bitchy and sarcastic and funny, and she constantly ate the last of my ice cream and never replaced it. She was always there to listen to me. She was always up for a good time and loved to have fun. She loved life, she lived it to the fullest. That's what I'm going to remember. Those are the things I will keep in my heart. One day when I'm not mad as all fuck at the world I'll tell you about all her shitty attempts at making homemade pumpkin pie. I'll tell you about the time she caught her car on fire. She was crazy, she did the craziest shit, and she breezed through life with the most beautiful smile. She didn't believe in marriage, but she believed in love. She didn't want a funeral. She didn't want a memorial service. She didn't want her ashes buried or scattered. She never told me why and I never asked because that was Elise —she lived her life on her terms, period. And I'll miss her every day for the rest of my life. That's how I'm doing this morning. But don't be shocked if in two hours from now I'm bawling my eyes out and I'll need you to hold me again."

He met my long-winded soliloquy with complete and utter silence. Not only that but Asher was stone-still under me. I didn't squirm, I didn't start to panic, I didn't wind myself up and let my mind wander. This was Asher—my Asher. I didn't need him to say anything. I could feel his strong arms around me. I could feel him readying himself to shield me from all the pain that I had bottled up in my chest.

I relaxed into him and waited.

Though he didn't make me wait long.

"You amaze me," he whispered. "Totally and completely undo me. I thought it was your hope that made me fall in love with you. But now I'm thinking it's your honesty. But the thing about you is, I know that tomorrow or the next day you'll do something or say something or show me a new side to you and I'll think that's the reason I love you. With you, the possibilities are endless. They're endless and so fucking beautiful."

Did he just...did he just say...he loves me?

I didn't know it was possible to have a broken heart while at the same time that same heart was so full of happiness.

"You love me?"

"Yup."

"I just asked if you loved me and you *yupped* me?"

"Were you hoping I'd say no, I didn't love you?"

"No, I was hoping you'd tell me you loved me again."

"I love you."

"I love you, too." Since my cheek was still resting on his chest I heard and felt him suck in a breath and I smiled. "There's something else you should know."

"What's that, baby?"

"I don't care how fast it is, I don't care who thinks we're crazy, but I'm moving to Idaho. I'm living my life on my terms. I'm living it to the fullest and I'm doing it by your side. I want to help you finish your house. I want to visit Letty's bookstore. I want to watch Brooklyn record more chapters. I want to get to know Mrs. Simpson. I want to stuff my stomach full of lemon poppyseed muffins. I want to meet the rest of your friends. I want to learn how to ski. I want to go fishing with you. I want to have a ton of kids and grow old with you. And the reason I don't have to care, the reason I'm able to throw caution to the wind and follow my heart is because I know you'll be there to protect my heart."

Asher loosened his arms and rolled us to the side so we were face-to-face.

"You're moving to Idaho? In here with me?"

"Yup."

He slowly blinked then pushed the top of his head into my chest and busted out laughing. His body shook so hard with it that I shook right along with him. The only thing better would've been if I could've seen him smiling. But the absolute best was—I could feel his happiness.

———

IT HAD TAKEN a lot to talk Asher into taking me to Wilson's condo. But after our heart-to-heart, Asher informed me the girls were waiting for me to call them and if I waited much longer before I reached out to them, they'd show up like they did the other day. Once again Asher was right. I called Letty and she informed me she and River were on their way over to Asher's. The problem with that was Asher didn't have any furniture. At the same time, Asher was on the phone with Wilson and he suggested everyone meet at his condo since it was centrally located. That was the part I had to talk Asher into. He didn't want me to have to leave the house. But once I reminded him I was living my life to the fullest and that did not include me shutting myself away even on a bad day, he relented.

Now I was standing in front of a huge wall of windows

looking out over Lake Coeur d'Alene admiring all the beauty before wondering how in the world this was my life. Asher stepped behind me and pulled me back, his arms went around me, and I remembered—*Asher*.

He was the reason I was now looking out over a beautiful lake surrounded by good people.

"You ready?"

He wanted to know if I was ready to call Mr. and Mrs. Keller. They were waiting on my call. That was the only detail he'd told me. And the more I thought about it, that truly was the only detail I wanted. I never, ever wanted to know the rest.

"Yeah, I'm ready."

He guided me to the couch fully prepared to catch me if I should stumble. But I wasn't going to crumble. I was going to take everything Elise gave me over the years and hold on to it. I was going to find strength in memories.

I saw Letty and Brooklyn sitting close together on the loveseat, then I found Sadie sitting on the arm of the chair Reese was in.

It was then I realized I'd also find strength in new memories. None of them would ever replace Elise. But that was the beauty of friendship—you didn't have to shift one out to bring one in, there was plenty of room. Brooklyn and Letty were proof. They'd been best friends since forever, but they'd made room for Sadie. And now they'd made room for me.

Another stitch.

I took the phone from Asher and fought an eyeroll when I saw he'd already punched in the number. All I needed to do was hit send.

I closed my eyes and remembered Elise pacing the apartment with her phone glued to her ear, gabbing with her mom. I remembered her reading me some joke her dad sent as she cracked up hysterically.

I opened my eyes and hit send.

Two rings later I heard, "Hello?"

My heart seized and my hands started shaking. Before I knew what was happening Brooklyn was off the loveseat and on her knees in front of me, Letty wasn't far behind, and Sadie squeezed in next to me.

"Mrs. Keller, it's Sloane."

"Sloane," she breathed, and it was a good thing I warned Asher I might be bawling my eyes out again because there I was two hours later unable to hold back the tears.

Brooklyn pried my fist open and threaded our fingers together. I had no idea what I wanted to say to Elise's mom, so I blurted out the first thing that came to my mind.

"Elise loved you so much."

I heard Mrs. Keller's breath hitch and I didn't know if that was good or bad, but I had more to say.

"Did you know she used to iron my sheets? She told me that you told her the best night's sleep happened on ironed sheets, so the crazy girl would iron my sheets after I washed them. She used to tell me that the best part of growing up was having you and Mr. Keller as parents."

I paused to catch my breath before I went on. "I loved her so much. She was a good friend, the best. You and Mr. Keller taught her that so thank you. Thank you for sharing her with me."

"Sloane? Mr. Keller here. We want you to know something, too." His voice was deep and full of emotion. "Our Elise, she loved you, too. She talked about you all the time. But you know that, don't you?"

"Yes, sir, I know."

Sadie pitched sideways and leaned heavily into my side.

Letty scooted closer so her arm was brushing my shin. Surrounded. Totally surrounded by love.

My gaze lifted off my lap and locked onto Asher. His face was full of love and compassion. And if I was being completely honest, there was a healthy dose of annoyance in there, too. He wanted to be the one holding me close. But he stood back, giving me the gift of the girls' friendship.

I loved him all the more for it.

"I hate to bring this up, but her room is how she left it. I'm out of town right now but when I get back to California would you like me to—"

"Keep it."

"What?"

"You knew my girl best. What would she say about her *stuff*?"

This part hurt. This was the one thing I wasn't sure I could give Elise.

"She'd say to throw it in the trash. Stuff is stuff and all it does is weigh you down."

"We have all we need of her, Sloane. And if you think about it, so do you."

But I wanted more.

"She gave me a lot," I admitted.

"You keep what you want. Please donate the rest."

I decided my best course of action was to agree and think about it later.

"Thank you."

"No, thank *you*, Sloane."

With that, he hung up.

I sucked back the last of my tears.

And since I needed something good, something to be happy about, something to celebrate, I announced, "I'm moving to Idaho."

"Seriously?" Sadie asked and bumped my shoulder.

"Yup."

"Yay!" Brooklyn squeezed my hand.

But it was Letty's response that startled me. She dropped her head onto my knee and burst into tears.

"Don't mind her," Brooklyn started. "She's pregnant and emotional but she's pretending... well, not pretending, she's hiding it because she hasn't told her parents yet that she and River went behind everyone's back and got married in Vegas. She thinks that's a secret, too, but it's not. River hasn't told his siblings yet either. I don't know who I'm more afraid of—River's sister, Shiloh, or Letty's mom, Tally."

I felt Letty shaking and I was growing concerned that she was going to hyperventilate from crying so hard when I heard the giggle.

"Are you freaking serious?" Sadie snapped.

"C'mon, you knew she was pregnant. She hasn't had a drink in like three months," Brooklyn volleyed.

"Of course, I knew she was knocked up. But all this time I felt bad for eloping, and she did, too."

I glanced around the room and found all of the men were smiling. They knew Letty and River had gotten married.

Oh, by the way, River...he was like the next size up in good-looking men. I'd never met a man as tall as he was in real life. And his eyes were the bluest of blue. He and Letty were going to have a beautiful baby.

"Sorry," Letty muttered against my leg.

"You're not sorry," Sadie snapped then she looked at her husband with narrowed eyes. "You knew!"

Reese smartly didn't confirm nor deny.

River looked completely unfazed by Sadie's snit and totally content.

Cole was pinching his lips, no doubt to keep a smart-ass comment at bay.

Rhode was staring at Brooklyn while his shaking his head but he, too, was smiling.

I didn't know Jack and Davis beyond the helloes we'd exchanged but they looked amused at Letty's antics.

It was Wilson's gaze that held me captive. When I'd met him, he'd been friendly. The next time I saw him, he didn't look all that happy. But right then, he was smiling at me. But that wasn't what had fascinated me. It was the wink he gave me before he transferred his stare to Asher.

24

"WHEN ARE the movers picking up Sloane's stuff?" Rhode asked from the doorway of my office.

"Tomorrow, they go over there to pack. The next day, it'll be on its way."

"You still need to store the furniture in my outbuilding?"

All of my furniture was being stored on one side of my garage and the rest was in a small shed. In the last three weeks, Sloane and I had made progress on the living room but it was nowhere near furniture-ready yet.

"Yeah, if that's still cool."

"You know it is. I was just wondering because Brook had..."

Rhode trailed off when my office phone rang.

"Who the hell is calling you on the landline? Who even has that number?"

That was a good question. One that was easily solved.

I reached over and hit the speakerphone button hoping that answered the question.

"Hello?"

"Is this Adam Newcomb?"

My eyes shot to Rhode as he was yanking his phone out of his pocket.

"Who's this?"

"I met you awhile back at the club."

"Who. Is. This?" I demanded.

"I sat in a meeting with you and Will."

Fear seared through me. I grabbed my cell off my desk and pulled up my text messages, easily finding Sloane's name.

"Will who?"

The man blew out a breath, and through the silence, I sent Sloane a message asking her where she was.

Cole and Davis entered my office, both on high alert.

"Listen, Newcomb...or is it Noble? I'm calling you as a professional courtesy. Evans caught wind that Lorenzo turned. He's pissed and looking for retribution. Since Take-back had a part in takin' down Lorenzo, my guess is he's headed your way."

Cole darted out of my office. Davis stepped closer to my desk and Rhode continued to hold his phone close to my desk phone. Obviously, he'd called Wilson and had him on speaker.

"Mind telling me what you mean by professional courtesy?"

"Do you really want to waste time asking a stupid question you know the answer to? Or do you want the plate number of the last known car Evans was driving?"

"What's the plate?"

The man rattled off the number while I wrote it down. It wasn't until I went to set the pen down that I noticed how badly I was shaking.

I checked my phone. No text back from Sloane.

"How long we got until he gets here?"

"Don't know. He lost his tail and some wires got crossed on our end. It's been two days since anyone's laid eyes on him."

"Two fucking days!" I exploded.

Jesus fuck, he could be roaming around CDA right now with Sloane out there unprotected.

"Listen closely," I growled. "I don't know who you are, but I know I didn't like your vibe. Unless you give me something right now, if I see you up here, I'm shooting your ass. Fuck your professional courtesy."

"Jerry says he hopes you still have the bunny suit."

The line went dead, and I was momentarily stunned.

"What did that mean?" Wilson asked from Rhode's phone.

"Means he's DEA. When I was with the FBI I had a long-term assignment. I was undercover for nine months in a joint operation with the DEA. My partner's name was Jerry Mench. There was a running joke that working at the mall as the Easter Bunny would've been a better gig. When I left the FBI he sent me a bunny suit."

"Well, fuck me," Wilson seethed. "I'll make some calls and hit you back."

I was out of my chair grabbing my keys when I looked at Rhode. "Did you text River?"

"Yup, he's on his way."

"I'm not sticking around here waiting. The girls were headed to the Christmas tree farm."

"Then he's on his way to the farm."

"I'm riding with you," Davis announced and followed us down the hall.

"I need you to drive," I admitted.

Wordlessly, we jogged through the parking lot to Davis's truck. We quickly piled in and Davis peeled out.

I alternated between calling and texting. I couldn't see what Rhode was doing behind me but I'd bet he was doing the same thing—trying to get ahold of Brooklyn.

The next fifteen minutes were fucking torture. Pure goddamn hell. The last three weeks played through my mind. Sloane smiling and happy puttying walls. Sloane on her knees doing her best to sand the floors, fucking them up, and trying again. Her whispering in the dark, telling me stories about Elise. Sloane laughing on the phone with one of her girls. Meeting Remington for the first time and watching her fall in love with the kid. Decorating our disaster of a house for Christmas and insisting we get a tree even though there was nowhere to sit downstairs to enjoy it.

I couldn't lose her.

I was going to fucking kill Will Evans.

25

"SLOANE," Brooklyn hissed from beside me.

"Listen to me, you and Letty are running back to the front. I'm gonna take off to the back. He wants me. Stay in the trees."

"We're not leaving you."

"Letty is pregnant. Take her and go."

"Sloane."

"Serious as shit, right now, girlfriend, we do not have time to argue about this. This guy is a bad guy. A very bad guy. Please take Letty and go call for help."

My heart was pounding so hard in my chest that I was worried I was going to have a heart attack. I needed Letty and Brooklyn gone and safe so I could figure out how to evade Will. My only advantage was he wasn't dressed for the weather. His thin coat would only keep him warm out here for so long. Plus he wasn't wearing a hat.

Speaking of, I pulled my beanie farther down over my ears and wished I'd brought earmuffs as well, though when I'd put on my outfit I hadn't planned on running through a tree farm playing hide and seek with a disgusting pig.

"Okay. I'll take her, but only so I can call for help."

Thank you, God.

"Stay in the trees," I reminded her.

"Be safe."

"Promise."

Brooklyn dashed to the tree Letty was hiding behind. As soon as I saw her grab Letty's hand and run I stepped out from behind the tree into the clearing. For this to work, I needed Will's attention on me. There were a few issues with my plan. One, I didn't know if Will's partner was with him. And the other problem was I had no idea what the partner looked like. I never saw him, I only heard him.

I waited a few seconds, then took off running in the opposite direction from the girls, staying visible for now.

I heard snow crunching behind me and picked up my speed, careful not to slip on the ice. I zipped behind a tree, stumbled, but didn't go down. The girls should've been far enough ahead of me that I could double back and run toward the front of the farm to safety.

Another one of those pesky problems was that we'd walked nearly a mile looking for the perfect tree and there was no way I could run a mile in the snow, not even when I was in fear for my life. My legs were already burning, and my lungs were on fire. I was lucky I'd lasted this long and I knew it was only because if he caught me, death would be the least of my worries.

I'd be sold.

And Asher would scorch the earth to find me. He'd drag his teammates along for the ride and poor Remy would grow up without a daddy. I couldn't let that happen.

I have to run.

The footsteps were getting closer.

I just have to run.

Letty and Brooklyn would call the guys.

I pumped my legs faster, blinked away the tears in my eyes from the cold air battering my face, and ran as fast as I could.

Unfortunately, it wasn't fast enough.

I hit the ground with a thud, Will on my back. The wind was knocked out of me and my vision blurred.

No. This couldn't happen.

Will scrambled to his feet, grabbed a fistful of my hair, and yanked me to my feet. My beanie fell off and my ears were instantly numb.

Did I pick the coldest day in Idaho to go Christmas tree shopping?

"Playtime's over," Will snarled.

The hair-pulling was a low blow. He had total control over my head, and unless I wanted to be scalped, I had no choice but to follow.

"What are you doing here, Will?"

"I have to admit, you had me fooled. For months you worked at the club and I had no idea you were Elise's roommate. I just thought you were some broke bitch prude who needed a job. Lorenzo, the dumbfuck, should've checked you out. But that was my mistake, trusting the motherfucker. He cost me a lot of money. Him and that boyfriend of yours."

Oh, shit.

Oh, fuck.

Will was walking fast, using my hair like a leash. If he made it to the back of the farm the forest was so thick back there no one would find us. At least on the farm, there was a chance someone would see us, and Asher would definitely see the footprints in the snow.

"Are you lost?" I asked him.

"No, I'm not fucking lost."

"I think you are. You didn't see the sign back here. It's private property. You know people in Idaho shoot trespassers."

I didn't know if that was true or not but now, I hoped it was.

"Shut the fuck up, there was no sign."

The woods were coming up fast. I was out of time. I had to do something now.

So what if I lost some hair, right? It would grow back and it was better than following Will into the woods.

I dug my feet into the snow, jerked to a stop, and screamed out in pain as my scalp felt like it was being ripped off my skull.

"Shut the fuck up!"

Will turned and now was my chance.

I lunged for him. My right hand went to his groin. I grabbed his balls, though I was fairly certain I'd captured his dick in my grip, too. I squeezed as hard as I could, ignoring Will's high-pitched squeal. I kept squeezing and added the twist. Will's face turned pale and I twisted more, waiting until I felt them pop, but I was wearing gloves so maybe they'd already popped. Just to be certain I adjusted my grip and squeezed again.

Will crumpled to the ground, landing on his side. I saw a gun tucked under his coat. I quickly reached down to grab it.

And that was a good thing since a tall, dark-haired man stepped out from behind a tree.

I swung the barrel in his direction, and he wisely lifted his hands.

"You okay, Sloane?"

Shit, motherfucker, goddamn, he's voice number two.

Houston, I have a major problem. I was wearing thick ski gloves; I could barely get a gloved finger into the trigger guard and I had no idea if the safety was on. Asher had only taken me shooting once.

"Step back," I warned.

"I'm not here to hurt you."

"Sure, you're not."

"Listen, I called Asher. He's on his way."

Asher, not Adam.

"I don't know who you're talking about."

"Right. Okay. How about this? I'm gonna step back and you're not gonna shoot me."

That sounded like a really great plan considering I wasn't very confident I'd hit him with a bullet even with only five feet separating us.

"Maybe I want to shoot you. Maybe I wanna shoot your balls off for threatening to kidnap Sammy. Who'd you take in her place?"

The man's eyes narrowed. "You did hear."

"Damn right I heard, you pig."

"I'm not gonna hurt you. As soon as Asher gets here, he'll explain everything. But please don't shoot my balls off." He smiled.

Did he think this was a joke?

"Sloane!" I heard Asher yelling my name.

Thank God.

"Over here!" I yelled back.

I kept my eyes on the man and the gun aimed in his direction while I waited for Asher to get to me.

"Sloane, sweetheart, you're shaking. Lower the gun."

He was right, I was shaking. I was freezing cold.

"Fuck off."

I saw Asher dart through a grouping of trees and come into the clearing.

"Jesus Christ!" I heard him yell and he started running full-out.

Behind him were Cole and Davis.

Asher got to me, grabbed the gun, and looked down at Will. What was going on?

"That's Will's partner," I warned Asher.

Asher's face turned a scary shade of red.

"Thought you said you didn't have eyes on him," he told the man.

"I didn't. I had eyes on Sloane. He showed up about a minute after I called you."

Wait, what the hell was going on?

Cole came to stand on the other side of me and Davis bent down to look Will over.

"And you didn't think to call me back? Or better yet, tell me you had eyes on my woman?"

"I was a little busy chasing three women hopping from tree to tree while I was trying to keep a location on that motherfucker. Plus, there's no goddamn service out here or I would've called for backup."

Backup?

A loud, agonized sob came from the ground. We all looked down at Will. His eyes were still closed, he was motionless, but he was crying.

"What happened to him?" Cole asked.

"I busted a nut, that's what happened," I announced. "Though there was no popping, so I kept twisting. His face went pale and he went down so I guess I did it right. Oh, and I think I got some of his dick in the grab portion of the grab, squeeze, and twist."

"Come again?" Davis asked.

"I busted a nut. You know, popped his balls. Broke his dick off. Whatever you wanna call it."

Then suddenly all four men's laughter rang out.

It was loud and they did it for a very long time.

Asher was the first to settle and when he did he pulled me into his arms and kissed my forehead.

"Proud of you, baby."

"Thanks. I was going to shoot that guy, but I couldn't reach the trigger with my gloves on."

"Thank God for that," the guy grumbled. "Though after hearing what you did to Will, I'd take the bullet wound over the nut-busting."

"Who are you?" I asked.

The man looked at Asher, then down at Will and finally his gaze came back to me.

"My name's Tim."

"Who's taking him in?" Asher asked.

"You."

"You're still under?"

Again I was totally lost but I was so damn cold I didn't care what they were talking about as long as they hurried the hell up so Asher could take me home. I needed a hot shower and a cup of coffee.

"Twenty months and counting."

"Jesus."

"You know how it is." Tim shrugged and smiled at me. "Sorry to hear about Elise. I was holding out hope for you."

"You knew Elise?"

"No, but I knew why you were there. Good friends like you are hard to come by."

Without saying goodbye, Tim turned and walked away.

"What just happened?"

Asher leaned close and whispered, "He's DEA."

"Seriously?"

"Yup."

Holy shit. I almost shot an undercover DEA agent.

Thank God I was wearing my ski gloves.

"Do I need to wait around for Will to come-to? I'm freezing and I want to check on Letty and Brooklyn."

"They're with Rhode and River."

Okay, that was good.

"Can you walk me back or can Cole? I think my blood is turning to ice and I still need to finish decorating."

"Sloane, baby, you were just stalked and chased through a tree farm and you wanna get home to decorate?"

"I was stalked, chased, tackled, and I busted a nut. But now that you mention it, before I decorate I'm gonna take a nice, long, hot bath."

"Baby."

Asher was giving me my favorite look. The one where his face went gentle, and his eyes were soft. He gave it to me a lot. Usually, after I'd done something to make him laugh. And thankfully he laughed a lot. But he was easy like that.

"Baby what?"

"That's another reason. They just keep coming."

He was talking about the reasons why he loved me.

I didn't ask what his new reason was. Sometimes he told me, sometimes he didn't. But like with all things Asher, I didn't need him to tell me, because he always made sure I felt his love. And in return, I made sure he felt mine.

"MORNING." I felt the word rumble against the back of my neck.

I came fully awake and smiled.

Naked, Asher curled into my back, our legs tangled.

The perfect way to wake up.

"Morning," I returned, and with great effort, I ignored the temptation of Asher's erection pressing on my ass. "Hold that thought."

I rolled to my nightstand and opened the drawer. We'd agreed, no presents. So instead of Christmas wrapping paper, the box was wrapped in lime green and white polka dot paper.

See? Not a Christmas present.

I rolled back, twisted, and held out the smallish box between us.

Asher's eyes dropped to the present, his lips twitched, and he muttered, "Couldn't help yourself, could you?"

No, I couldn't.

"Open it."

Asher sat up and scooted until his back was against the headboard.

The blanket fell away and pooled on his lap. And like all the times before when his chest was presented to me, I never missed an opportunity to take it in.

So damn hot.

"Baby, do you want me to open your present or fuck you?"

I didn't move my eyes from his pecs when I answered.

"Both."

It was his laughter that made me drag my eyes up to watch.

I'd been wrong, *this* was the perfect way to wake up—naked in bed with Asher laughing.

He pitched to the side, opened his nightstand drawer, and pulled out a gift wrapped in dinosaur birthday paper.

I fell to my back and busted out laughing.

"Great minds," I sputtered through my giggles.

I felt the box land on my stomach followed by, "Open it."

I picked it up and immediately knew what it was.

I sat up, let the comforter fall away, and shivered when I heard Asher's growl of appreciation.

So what if I bared my breasts on purpose? My man liked me naked, and I loved hearing him growl like a caveman. Besides, it was Christmas morning.

"You first," I told him, vibrating with excitement.

Asher did as asked and I knew when he smiled he'd opened the present right side up so he could see the photo in the frame.

"You like it?"

He didn't answer, not with words—his shoulders shook and his laughter filled our bedroom.

"I...fucking..." he choked out, "love it."

I knew he would.

An eight-by-ten framed picture of Caitlyn O'Leary and her husband John. Signed of course by John, not Caitlyn. And John had added a note: *To Asher, the founding member of the John O'Leary fan club.*

"Now you."

I tore open the paper knowing by its shape it was a book. But when the paper came free and I saw it was my favorite Caitlyn book, I shouted my joy.

"I love it!"

"Open the book."

I flipped it open and saw Caitlyn had signed it and under her signature, John had left his own note: *Sloane, I hope to meet you at the inaugural fan club get-together. - John.*

"They probably think we're crazy," I said and closed the book.

"Baby, we *are* crazy."

That we were, and I still didn't give two shits.

"Thank you for my book."

"Thank you for my autographed John picture."

He leaned over, set the frame on his nightstand, tagged the book from my hand, and set it on top of the frame. And when he was done with that, he came down over the top of me.

"Happy first Christmas, baby."

"Happy first Christmas, Asher."

His lips brushed over mine and he murmured, "I love you."

I didn't get a chance to say it back before his tongue pushed into my mouth and he kissed me breathless. A few minutes after that he commenced fucking me senseless. It wasn't until much later after Christmas orgasms had been had and my head was on his chest, our legs tangled, my arm resting over his stomach, that I finally got to reply.

"I love you more than breath."

26

Cole Keniston

I peeled one eye open and squinted at my alarm. 3:07. Nothing good comes from the phone ringing at three in the morning. I tagged my phone off my nightstand, praying to all things holy it wasn't Wilson telling me we were rolling out.

Unknown caller.

Fuck.

"'Lo," I grumbled.

"Cole."

The sound of my name rushing out from an old friend had me rolling up on my elbow.

"Pete? What's wrong?"

"Fuck, Cole, I need a favor."

A favor at three in the morning from a Navy buddy could mean anything from bail money to needing a shovel and manpower. I was hoping it was the former. Dirty work wasn't my favorite.

"Whatcha need?"

"I need you to stash my sister."

What the fuck?

"Why do you sound out of breath?"

"Because I'd prefer not to get dead tonight."

I swung my legs over the edge of the bed and was up looking for pants when I asked, "Where are you?"

"Mexico."

"What the fuck are you doing in Mexico?"

Pete left the Navy the year after I did. Last I talked to him he was selling real estate.

"Listen, I don't have time to explain. Can you take Mia?"

I froze in the middle of my bedroom and hung my head.

Why did it have to be Mia? Why not his sweet baby sister Camilia?

"Of course," I ground out. "Where do I need to pick her up?"

"As soon as we get back to Texas tonight I'm getting her on the first flight out."

Tomorrow, Mia Young would be back in my life and in my house.

"Does Mia know she's comin' to me?"

"It was her suggestion. And you're the only one stateside I trust."

Right, Mia was back at her old tricks.

Unfortunately for her, I wasn't the same twenty-two-year-old idiot she used to know.

"Send me her flight info and make sure she has my number. I'll get her tomorrow."

"Thanks, brother, I owe you one."

Pete disconnected before I could remind him he owed me about twenty.

I tossed my phone back on my nightstand and climbed back into bed. I lay there in the dark wondering who I pissed off, or what bad deed I'd done to warrant such a cruel and unusual punishment. I knew if I thought about it hard enough, I could still feel her soft body pressed against mine. And if I really wanted to torture myself, I could recall her sweet voice whispering 'I love you' in my ear right before she walked away.

Next up is Cole and Mia in Dangerous Mind

AUDIO

Are you an Audio Fan?

Check out Riley's titles in Audio on Audible and iTunes

Gemini Group

Narrated by: Joe Arden and Erin Mallon

Red Team

Narrated by: Jason Clarke and Carly Robins

Gold Team

Narrated by: Lee Samuels and Maxine Mitchell

The 707 Series

Narrated by: Troy Duran and C. J. Bloom

More audio coming soon!

ALSO BY RILEY EDWARDS

Riley Edwards

www.RileyEdwardsRomance.com

Takeback

Dangerous Love

Dangerous Rescue

Dangerous Games

Dangerous Encounter

Dangerous Mind

Gemini Group

Nixon's Promise

Jameson's Salvation

Weston's Treasure

Alec's Dream

Chasin's Surrender

Holden's Resurrection

Jonny's Redemption

Red Team - Susan Stoker Universe

Nightstalker

Protecting Olivia

Redeeming Violet

Recovering Ivy

Rescuing Erin

The Gold Team - Susan Stoker Universe

Brooks

Thaddeus

Kyle

Maximus

Declan

Blue Team - Susan Stoker Universe

Owen

Gabe

Myles

Kevin

Cooper

Garrett

The 707 Freedom Series

Free

Freeing Jasper

Finally Free

Freedom

The Next Generation (707 spinoff)

Saving Meadow

Chasing Honor

Finding Mercy

Claiming Tuesday

Adoring Delaney

Keeping Quinn

BE A REBEL

Riley Edwards is a USA Today and WSJ bestselling author, wife, and military mom. Riley was born and raised in Los Angeles but now resides on the east coast with her fantastic husband and children.

Riley writes heart-stopping romance with sexy alpha heroes and even stronger heroines. Riley's favorite genres to write are romantic suspense and military romance.

Don't forget to sign up for Riley's newsletter and never miss another release, sale, or exclusive bonus material.

Rebels Newsletter

Facebook Fan Group

www.rileyedwardsromance.com

📘 facebook.com/Novelist.Riley.Edwards

📷 instagram.com/rileyedwardsromance

BB bookbub.com/authors/riley-edwards

a amazon.com/author/rileyedwards

ACKNOWLEDGMENTS

To all of you – the readers: Thank you for picking up this book and giving me a few hours of your time. Whether this is the first book of mine you've read or you've been with me from the beginning, thank you for your support. It is because of you I have the coolest job in the world.

Made in United States
Orlando, FL
16 September 2022

22455035R20150